Markus Reussmin is a wolf shifter who's worked as a Stone Ridge deputy for over a decade. Over the last couple of years, he's had a few people comment on how he doesn't look as if he's aged a day, but he's always laughed it off as good genes. After all, he isn't ready to go into hiding so he can reappear after a decade with a new reinvention of himself.

When the sheriff's department receives a report of smoke in a remote part of the forest, Markus is dispatched to check it out. He hikes into the area and discovers a rudimentary campsite. That's not all. The site is occupied by none other than his mate . . . judging by the delicious scent pervading the area.

With the help of his shifter nose, Markus locates the hiding human — Ronan Dyer — who turns out to be wary and untrusting of law enforcement. That makes sense, since he's hiding from the government. Can Markus convince the skittish human he's not the bad guy so he can help him, even as he explains the complexities of shifters and matings before his pack's mountains are invaded by government stooges?

Winning the Survivalist
Copyright © 2021 Charlie Richards
ISBN: 978-1-4874-3186-0
Cover art by Angela Waters

Published by eXtasy Books Inc or
Devine Destinies, an imprint of eXtasy Books Inc

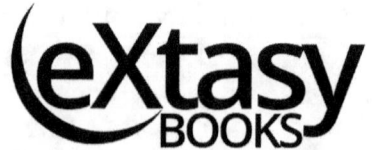

Look for us online at:
www.eXtasybooks.com or www.devinedestinies.com

Winning the Survivalist

Wolves of Stone Ridge Book Fifty-Four

By

Charlie Richards

DEDICATION

Every great move forward in your life begins with a leap of faith, a
step into the unknown.
~Unknown

CHAPTER ONE

Whistling softly, Markus Reussmin strolled down the street. He peered around town, taking in the morning bustle. All around him, Stone Ridge was coming to life, and he loved watching it.

Shopkeepers waved to each other as they unlocked their doors. There were several parents holding their young children's hands as they escorted them into the elementary school. Even a couple of brave souls sat at outdoor tables drinking coffee and exchanging gossip.

Miss Martha's Muffins was already in full swing, and the delicious aroma of pastries and hot coffee pervaded the street. He knew many of the parents would pass through their doors after dropping off their youngsters. It was a hot spot for locals to catch up on the latest news. As he passed the bakery, the bells on the door of the small shop jingled as a customer hurried inside, getting out of the spring chill.

"Yoo-hoo! Deputy!"

Turning to look back, Markus spotted Miss Martha herself — who was really Misses Martha Warren — standing in the doorway. The middle-aged woman's husband had passed away three years before. Her shop had been her saving grace, keeping her occupied and surrounded by supportive friends, family, and townspeople.

According to the local gossip, Martha had even been making noise about starting to date again.

Markus wished her well in her search for a new husband.

Martha held up a cup of coffee and wiggled it. "Coffee,

Deputy?" Then she must have spotted the travel mug Markus carried in his left hand, for her features morphed into a teasing pout as she started toward him. "So that's why you didn't come in." Then she lifted her other hand, which held a small paper sack. "But surely you don't want to skip out on a morning bear claw?"

Taking the few steps necessary to reach her, Markus smiled at the blonde-haired woman. While she was a little overweight, probably from enjoying a few too many of her wares, she had a friendly smile. Her brown eyes glimmered with happiness, and her cheeks were a rosy color, maybe from baking.

"Thank you, Miss Martha," Markus stated, reaching for the bag. "That's awful nice of you. I'll be in to pay for it on my lunch break."

"Oh, don't you even worry about that," Martha responded, shaking her head. "How about I meet up with you for your lunch instead?"

Well, fuck. Guess those guys passing on the rumors were actually warning me.

"I appreciate the thought, Miss Martha," Markus began slowly, racking his brain for a nice way to let the human down. "But I never know where I'm going to end up during the day or even what time lunch could end up being."

As a wolf shifter, he knew by scent that she wasn't his mate. He had no desire to lead her on, since Fate could bring his mate to him at any moment. Besides, he preferred male company to female, not that he advertised that since he didn't date . . . anyone.

No point.

For a second, disappointment creased her features. It disappeared almost instantly to be replaced by a beaming smile. "Well, since you're so busy, you should let me know what time you get off work. It sounds like you could use a home-cooked meal." When Martha swept her gaze over Markus's frame, a definite gleam of interest lit her brown eyes. "Although, you don't look like you've aged a day in the last ten years." Meeting his gaze, Martha fluttered her eyelashes at him. "When you come over for dinner, you're gonna have to tell me your secret."

Markus chuckled uncomfortably. "Uh, well, I can tell you now," he told her. Before she could counter, he quickly added, "I keep a small herd of animals and have a large greenhouse. For the most part, I only eat what I butcher or grow." Holding up the bag, Markus smiled as he added, "Of course, your wonderful bear claws are the occasional exception." Then he turned and took a step in the other direction. "Thanks again, Miss Martha. I'll be in when I can to settle up. I gotta get on with my patrol now."

"Oh, of course." Martha moved to stand beside him once more, holding the coffee. "Did you want me to pour this into your travel mug? It's black, just how you like it."

"No thanks, Miss Martha," Markus declined. "My mug's still almost full." It was a good thing humans couldn't scent lies like shifters could. The mug was actually almost empty. "See you later, ma'am."

Markus hoped using honorifics would get his disinterest across.

No such luck.

Martha laughed and waved as she called, "Call me Martha, Markus. You're making me feel old."

"I'll try to remember that," Markus told her, although he recalled the other four times she'd told him that. *Guess that should have been a sign.* "Have a good morning."

Then Markus reached the crosswalk and hurried across, feeling relieved that there wasn't any traffic to hold him up. As he resumed his patrol, he placed the bag in his left hand, tucking it between a couple of fingers. That allowed him to hold the bag and mug at the same time. Markus needed his right hand free in case he needed to access the walkie-talkie on his shoulder . . . or his service weapon.

Of course, if that ever happened, Markus would just toss the stuff in his left hand and retrieve it later.

Markus would never tell Martha, but he didn't care for how she brewed her standard cup of coffee. Her iced lattes were good, however, but it was too cold for them. As he held the bag in his hand, he had to acknowledge that nothing beat her bear claws.

Well, maybe Brad's cinnamon buns, but I sure as hell would never tell her that.

Brad Nadeau was a polar bear shifter who ran a bakery in Colin City, a town almost forty-five minutes away on the windy mountain roads.

Markus still marveled at the changes that had happened in his wolf shifter pack over the last decade. They'd faced off against scientists, the government, and the shifter council. Each had varying results.

What impressed Markus the most was the fact that their wolf pack leader — Alpha Declan McIntire — hid nothing from his pack-members. He believed the adage that knowledge was power, and he armed his pack-members with it. Declan shared the basics of what was happening, so none of his people could be caught unawares.

On top of that, Declan also welcomed more than just wolf shifters into his territory. Not only was Brad in Colin City, which was right on the outskirts of the pack's territory, but so was a black panther shifter. Others that were local included an elephant shifter mated with one of their detectives — a tiger shifter. Another on the force was a monitor lizard shifter, although that last one was due to a scientific experiment gone awry. He'd originally been human.

To Markus's knowledge, Detective Lyle Sullivan was the only human ever to have been turned into a shifter.

After finishing his coffee, Markus looped a tiny bungee cord through the handle and attached it to his belt. He then pulled out the bear claw and threw away the paper sack in a garbage bin he passed. As he ate, he continued to check out the area.

Markus finished the sugary, doughy treat in five big bites. Licking his fingers, he realized just how much he appreciated his speedy shifter metabolism. As he'd prepared his steak, baked potato, and Brussel sprouts the evening before, he'd started thinking about cutting out most of the sweets from town.

And now with Martha asking me out, I'm going to have to avoid the damn place like the plague.

While wiping his damp fingertips on the leg of his jeans, Markus heard his microphone chirp to life. "This is dispatch. Come in, Deputy Reussmin."

Recognizing Michelle Laraby's voice, Markus fought the urge to roll his eyes. Only their station's receptionist could make it sound as if contacting him was beneath her while over the radio. He sometimes wondered if she had a stick up her ass all the time, or if it was just because she was working with a bunch of dominant males that caused her to decide she had to be a, well . . . a bitch. Markus wasn't certain. Michelle had been that way since the day he was hired on part time. He loved that he'd been able to join full time two years prior.

Maybe she just needs to get laid.

Markus pressed the transmit button on his microphone and replied, "This is Deputy Reussmin. Go ahead, dispatch."

"I've received three reports of smoke about a mile west of Hormel Peak trailhead. There's no camping in there," Michelle pointed out needlessly.

Markus already knew that.

Before Markus could reply, Michelle continued, "Sheriff Parkinson wants you to check it out."

"I'll be back at my vehicle in five minutes, dispatch," Markus replied, starting that way with ground-eating strides. "I'll be on the road shortly. How long ago were the reports?"

He didn't ask why it had taken three of them before the sheriff had decided to check it. Sheriff Blake Parkinson was getting on in years, but he kept putting off retirement because he feared a fag would replace him.

Not that Blake had actually said that in front of anyone. Markus had happened to overhear it just a few weeks ago. Blake had been on the phone, and his door had been cracked open—probably by accident.

Mental note, tell Alpha Declan about it.

Markus knew Declan would find a way to get a gay-friendly person in the office. Hell, it would probably end up being a shifter. Markus wondered if the honor would fall to one of the detectives.

"The first source wasn't credible. The second source said the fire faded as they watched," Michelle told him, answering his unspoken curiosity. "It wasn't until we received a call from Ranger Holsteen that Sheriff Parkinson decided there may be something to it."

Markus did roll his eyes then. Ranger Holsteen was actually Beta Dixon Holsteen, second-in-command of their wolf pack. If he'd noticed a fire, then there had to be some problem out there.

I wonder why the rangers aren't checking it then.

Unable to contain his curiosity a second time, Markus asked just that.

Michelle's derisive sniff was loud enough to come through the line. "Evidently, they're on a call about a missing hiker. They won't have anyone available for at least three hours, so they asked us to check it."

"Got it." As Markus approached his vehicle, he used his fob to unlock it. "I'm on it. I'll report back as soon as I can."

Markus slid behind the wheel before firing it up. Once he'd pulled the belt around himself, he checked his mirrors and eased out of the parking lot. Heading north out of town, Markus wondered what he would find.

While it was still technically the rainy season, a lightning strike could potentially start a forest fire. There was enough snow on the ground that it would fizzle swiftly, though. If several people saw it, there was a possibility of a poacher camping out there.

It had been years, but that didn't mean it was out of the realm of possibility. As wolf shifters, they patrolled their territory regularly, but they controlled a big area. Someone could have slipped through.

"If it *is* a poacher, I'll cross that bridge when I get to it," Markus murmured to himself.

As Markus drove deeper into the mountains, he noticed the size of the patches of lingering snow increasing. His vehicle's external temperature gauge ticked lower and lower. By the time he reached the area he needed, it read that it was thirty-seven degrees outside.

"Damn," Markus muttered. "If it really is a poacher, they're diehard about it."

Markus hoped he didn't find anyone.

Driving slowly away from the Hormel Peak trailhead parking area, heading west, Markus kept sweeping over the tops of the trees. He'd traveled nearly two miles along the winding road and was beginning to think it was a bogus call or the fire was already out. Except, that didn't seem like something his pack beta would do or make a mistake about.

With his faith in his pack beta driving him onward, Markus kept looking. He stopped after five miles and frowned. Turning this way and that in his seat, he tried to decide if he should turn around and make another pass or call Dixon to see if he could get a more specific location.

As much as he was loath to interrupt his beta while in the middle of a call, Markus didn't know if he was in the right area. He didn't really have faith in Sheriff Parkinson or Michelle to get their information right. The pair had been at the job so long, in a small town with very little crime, that they'd grown more than a little lax.

Part of that problem might be the fact that most of the past dangerous elements in town had been pack related, so they'd hidden it from the pair.

Just as Markus picked up his phone, a hint of gray to his left caught his attention. He rolled down his window, bracing himself against the cold air. Lifting his shades, he squinted as he looked over the pine treetops.

There, in the distance, was a thin wisp of smoke.

"Damn," Markus mumbled. "There's not supposed to be anything out there. It's state park property."

Rolling up his window, Markus pulled his vehicle onto the shoulder at the first safe place he found. He turned in his seat and grabbed his heavy deputy's coat from the back seat. After exiting his truck, he pulled on the thick fabric and zipped it.

Markus radioed in that he'd spotted the smoke and the mile marker where he'd roughly left his truck. Then he started into the forest.

As a wolf shifter, Markus didn't feel the cold quite as intensely as a human would. Hiking through the chilly mid-morning air, he was damn grateful for that. He didn't envy any human trying to camp in the mountains of Colorado in the spring.

Maybe it's a paranormal.

The random thought flitted through his brain. He supposed it was a possibility. That meant whoever it was would probably be on the run from someone.

"Let's not jump to conclusions," Markus muttered.

His imagination was getting away from him.

As much as Markus tried to be quiet, his boots crunched on the dead leaves, spots of snow, and wet branches littering the ground. He slowly weaved his way through the pines, keeping in the general direction he'd spotted the smoke. When his sensitive shifter nose picked up the hint of burning timber,

Markus knew he was getting close.

Finally, Markus ran across a deer trail heading in the right direction and began to follow it. He'd been on it for less than ten minutes when a small, ten-by-fifteen-foot clearing opened up before him. Seeing the set up within, he froze, his hand instinctively lowering to his service weapon.

There was a tent tucked under the boughs of a pine on the right, covered in a waterproof tarp. Boughs lined the base and bottom, providing extra warmth. A fire pit lined with rocks was five feet in front of the tent's opening. Someone had even fashioned a make-shift cover over it using sticks lashed together with twine and bark.

Markus felt the hairs on the back of his neck lift, the sensation telling him that he was being watched. Inhaling slowly, he swept his gaze over the area once more, searching. He didn't see anyone.

Except, the scent called to him on a primitive level he'd never before experienced. His blood heated in his veins, and his wolf urged him to track down the source.

Shock flooded him as realization set in.

Somewhere in these woods, hiding from me, is my mate. Just what the fuck could he be doing out here?

And where is he?

CHAPTER TWO

Ronan Dyer crouched behind a thick bush, peering through the branches. His left knee ached, but he didn't dare move to adjust his stance. He clenched his jaw, pushing the pain from his mind, just as he'd been taught in the military.

I can wait as long as it takes.

"This is Deputy Markus Reussmin," the uniformed officer called. "Is anyone here?"

Markus cocked his head a little, clearly listening. At the same time, he slowly panned his gaze over the clearing. He called a second time, then listened, before moving slowly toward Ronan's tent. All the while, Markus continued to look around the area.

Twice, Markus's attention paused at the bush where Ronan hid. To his relief, each time he kept searching. When he stopped at Ronan's tent, Marcus unzipped the flap and lifted it. He didn't enter, for which Ronan was grateful, but he must have noticed his small gas cook-stove and carefully sealed foodstuffs.

"Poacher or hunter?" Markus mused, clearly talking out loud.

Ronan curled his lip in annoyance. Of course, *that* would be what the deputy would assume. He figured it didn't matter. As soon as the man left, Ronan would pack up and move on.

No way could he stick around after getting noticed . . . especially by law enforcement.

Watching Markus straighten as he stepped away from his tent, Ronan found his gaze snagged by the deputy's jeans-clad ass. It was damn fine, after all — high and tight. His thighs filled out his jeans in the best way possible, and his waist appeared trim, although it was tough to tell about his torso under his thick jacket.

Shit! Stop checking out the deputy. So not the time.

Even with his mental admonishment, Ronan still felt his groin heat and his prick begin to swell. He rolled his eyes and just bit back his growl of annoyance. Having had longer dry-spells than three years, he would smack himself upside the head later.

To Ronan's relief, after fifteen minutes of exploring the clearing and checking out the footprints crisscrossing the area, Markus left.

Ronan waited as long as his left knee would allow before his aging body forced him to move.

Damn cold aggravating my war injury.

Gritting his teeth, Ronan slowly straightened from his stance. He grabbed a nearby tree and leaned against it. Then he lifted his left leg and slowly straightened and bent his leg a few times. It took a few repetitions, but the ache finally began to ebb.

When Ronan moved to put weight on it, he still couldn't help but limp a little. He made his way back to the clearing. On damn near silent footfalls, he moved to where the deputy had disappeared between the trees.

Nothing.

Ronan didn't believe that Markus had given up, though. Even a small-town deputy would have to report a camp in a national forest. He would bring others when he returned the next time.

While Ronan didn't know how long that would be, he couldn't wait. He'd hoped the secluded area would mean he had some time to hunt, fish, and replenish his stores . . . not to mention give him some time to think. Instead, Ronan realized nosey country folk must have noticed him.

Damn it.

Ronan turned toward his tent. In his mind, he calculated how quickly it would take to break camp, pack everything, and clear any trace of his having been there. He didn't want to leave any way for someone to track him.

Except, there, standing next to his tent, was Deputy Markus Reussmin.

Shit! How did I miss that he was circling my camp?

Tensing, Ronan mentally calculated the odds of running. He could replace everything in the tent — mostly. Except, he'd left his rifle in there, hidden under the blankets, since he'd just been scouting the area.

Knew I should have taken it.

"Please, don't run," Markus urged, his tenor voice a low soothing croon. Lifting his hands, palms out in a placating manner, he told him, "I'm here because people saw smoke, and this is a state park."

Markus swept his gaze over him, and for just a second, Ronan thought he spotted a flash of heat in his hazel eyes. Just as quickly it was gone, hidden behind a furrowed brow. The deputy swept his gaze over him, his expression turning concerned.

Ronan knew what he looked like — a homeless bum. He'd been on the run for so long that his clothes were in dire need of a wash or three. His skin felt as if he had dirt encrusted underneath it. Even Ronan's attempt at hygiene by using his boot knife to keep his head and face closely shorn seemed a waste of time sometimes.

Except, Ronan hated beards . . . and long hair. He had felt the same even before he'd joined the marines. After over two decades in the service, his desire for as little hair to hassle with had become ingrained.

"You look like you could use a hot shower and a warm

bed." A wry smile curved Markus's lips, and his hazel eyes took on a hint of a twinkle. He indicated his campsite. "Not that this doesn't look cozy and all, but I bet pizza and beer in front of a roaring fireplace wouldn't go amiss right now, huh?"

What the hell?

Ronan's confusion must have been clear as day, for Markus cocked his head and cleared his throat. "How about we start over . . . just like we were two guys in a bar?"

Then he took a step forward, causing Ronan to tense and shuffle back a half-step.

Freezing, Markus stared hard at him. "We can't work out what's going on between us if you won't talk to me." He held out his hand as if they were going to shake, even though they stood twenty paces apart. "I'm Markus Reussmin. What's your name?"

Maybe it was the oddity of the situation, but Ronan found himself responding. "Ronan."

Markus made a movement with his hand as if they were shaking hands. At the same time, he grinned broadly. "Nice to meet you, Ronan." He took another step forward. "Can I buy you a beer?"

Ronan couldn't help but mumble, "A beer?"

Is this guy playing with a full deck?

Nodding once, Markus rested his hands on his hips. "Sure. How else will we talk about what you're doing out here?"

Between Markus's words and his movements — which put his right hand damn close to his gun — Ronan jerked out of his confused shock. He took a step backward. He needed to get away from this guy who confused him — a guy who was also law enforcement.

"Don't run," Markus ordered again.

Except, this time, Ronan ignored him. He turned and lunged into the woods. Unfortunately, as soon as he put weight on his left knee, it buckled.

Ronan couldn't help his bark of surprise as he started to topple, grabbing a tree to stop his tumble.

Even before Ronan had managed to regain control, Markus was at his side, grabbing him, helping him catch his balance. Then he wrapped his arms around Ronan's waist, one around his belly and the other across his torso.

Markus hauled Ronan upright in a way that belied their differences in hulk. Even though he had a good inch or so on the deputy, the other man took his weight without trouble. He even nuzzled at Ronan's neck and murmured platitudes, promising he would be okay, that they would figure things out, and that he would help in any way he could.

Ronan stilled in Markus's hold. Even though he could think of several ways he could break out of the guy's grip, now that he had his feet under him and his knee was taking his weight, he didn't. Instead, he tried to figure out just what the hell was going on with the other man.

He sure as hell isn't behaving like any law enforcement officer I've ever run into.

Then an idea popped into his head. "If you think I'm going to give you drugs to let me go, it's not going to happen," he growled, scowling over his shoulder at Markus. "I don't do drugs, and I don't have any."

To Ronan's surprise, Markus grinned widely. "Good to know. I don't either." Then, boggling Ronan's mind even more, Markus pressed a kiss to his cheek. "Let's—"

"Dispatch to Deputy Reussmin." The radio on Markus's shoulder squealed to life. "Come in, Deputy Reussmin."

With a wink, Markus released Ronan with the arm around his torso, the one around his waist loosening, too. "This is Deputy Reussmin. Go ahead."

Ronan took advantage of Markus's distraction. Sprinting to his tent, he ignored whatever the dispatch lady was saying. He dove into his tent, which Markus had left partially open earlier. After a quick shove to his bedding, Ronan yanked up his rifle, rolled to his ass, and pointed the weapon out the tent flap.

Once again, confusion flooded Ronan. Markus was still where he'd left him, although his head was cocked and he peered in his direction. His expression remained calm even as he replied to whatever the woman had said.

"Yes, I found the source of the fire."

Ronan felt his gut twist, and he could practically feel the blood drain from his face.

Markus's eyes narrowed, but his voice remained steady as he continued, "It looks like a lightning strike from Thursday's storm set a couple of trees on fire. They're taking turns smoldering, but they're safe." After a heartbeat, Markus added, "I'm going to be taking my lunch break, since I'm in the neighborhood of my house. Let me know if the chief wants me back in town or somewhere else afterward."

"I'll close the reports then, Deputy," the woman replied. "The schedule I have here says you're to patrol the northern roads. We've had reports of boys joy-riding up there and putting other motorists in danger."

"Got it," Markus replied. "Deputy Reussmin out." Lowering his hand, he pinned a calm look on Ronan. "So, Ronan, how about I help you pack all this shit up and take you home for lunch?"

Slowly lowering his rifle, Ronan couldn't help but ask, "Why would you do that?"

Markus's lips curved into a hint of a smile. "Oh, Ronan. There are so many reasons, and I don't even know where to begin." Taking two steps forward before pausing again, he resumed talking before Ronan could come up with another question. "Here's what I'd like to do this afternoon. I'd like to help you pack everything up. You can't stay here. It's a state park." Markus used a thumb to point over his shoulder. "I'll help you carry it to my truck, unless you have one hidden around here somewhere?"

Ronan found himself shaking his head on instinct. He couldn't remember the last time that had happened.

"Damn," Markus murmured, his brows furrowing. "Hiked or hitchhiked way out here?" Shoving his hands into his jacket pockets, he took a few steps closer. "I can't even begin to guess at why you would need to do that. Are you homeless?"

Finding his tongue, Ronan muttered, "More or less."

Technically, his paychecks were direct deposited, and all his bills were paid electronically. Except, he couldn't access the money without alerting the authorities to his location.

Authorities like the man standing in front of me.

Ronan wished he could trust the handsome man before him, but he couldn't. He was a cop. From the way he'd lied to his own boss, he was a dirty one, to boot.

"Back away," Ronan ordered, even though the prospect of help was so damn appealing. "I don't want to hurt you. If you sit quietly, I'll pack up and leave. You'll never see me again."

A flicker of something passed over Markus's features—there and gone so fast Ronan couldn't follow it.

"I really wish I could get you to come with me willingly," Markus whispered.

Before Ronan could process the meaning of those words, Markus moved . . . faster than he thought anyone should have been able to. The deputy grabbed his rifle and yanked. Ronan's entire body was jerked forward as he attempted to hang on, but the other man was deceptively strong.

Ronan slid toward the door of the tent even as the weapon was pulled from his grip. His left foot caught on the bottom lip of the tent opening. As he tumbled forward, his leg twisted awkwardly.

Pain stabbed through his knee, forcing a gasp from between his lips. As his body folded over his legs and he landed on his knees, dark spots clouded his vision. Even as he struggled to breathe, slow and deep, trying to regain his control, he knew it was a losing battle.

Seconds later, Ronan flopped to his side as his body succumbed to the fiery agony.

CHAPTER THREE

Pacing the hallway, Markus glanced into the bedroom every time he passed the open doorway. He growled low under his breath, but he kept careful control and didn't go in. His alpha's mate, Lark Trystan, was checking Ronan's vitals . . . and his knee.

When Markus had discovered the amount of scarring on his human's appendage, he'd nearly roared with the need to find whoever had brutalized him so. It was a wonder the man could walk. He damn sure shouldn't be living in a tent in the middle of nowhere like some forgotten vagabond.

Markus hadn't known the extent of the damage, so when he'd cleaned his mate, he'd been extremely careful. Hell, he'd already hurt him enough to make him pass out. His wolf had driven him almost crazy with the need to correct his mistake, to make Ronan as comfortable as possible once he woke up.

To that end, Markus had stripped Ronan of his dirty clothes, rested him on the bench in his shower, and carefully washed him from head to toe. He'd avoided lingering, keeping his hands from caressing his gorgeous human as much as possible, since he'd known his actions could be taken as invasive, even if he was trying to help Ronan. Once his mate was clean, Markus had dried him, found a brand new pair of boxer-briefs that he'd acquired from somewhere — and couldn't remember when or where since he'd been going commando for decades — and had tucked him into the bed of his spare bedroom.

Then Markus had sat by his side, waiting for his alpha to

arrive with his mate, who was a doctor.

"No, Sheriff Parkinson. Deputy Markus will not be in for the rest of the afternoon. Unfortunately, ye won't be able to call in his brother, Deputy Ron, to cover for him either." Alpha Declan McIntire's deep, Irish-lilted voice pulled Markus out of his musing. As his alpha approached, his phone to his ear, a deep scowl marred his dark-skinned features. "That's right. They've had a family emergency. I wouldn't expect either of them for the rest of the week, to be honest." Declan's lips curled, but he kept the growl Markus could see building from within him out of his voice as he stated, "I can tell ye that because I'm the men's cousin, and their next of kin on emergency paperwork. The rest of their family is out of state, and that's where both men are headed right now."

With how close Declan had drawn to him, Markus could hear Sheriff Parkinson's response. "You tell Markus I want to hear this shit from him before his lunch hour is over, or he's fired!"

Even as Markus heard Declan growl, he couldn't resist grabbing the phone from his alpha's hand. "Then I'm fucking fired, you homophobic prick," he roared. Happy to have someone to take his frustration out on, he added, "And I plan to tell everyone who'll listen about your phone call with Sheriff Marston from the next county over." He scoffed as he added with a snarl, "Maybe you should make certain your door is closed before you start spouting off about how you won't step down until you're sure your job won't go to a fag!"

Before Markus could disconnect the call, Declan grabbed the phone back from him. He arched one brow in silent question as he said into the device, "That's why *I* called and not him," he claimed. "He's a wee bit emotional right now. It's his mother."

"Whatever," the sheriff grumbled. "Tell him he has the rest

of the week. Then I expect him back at work first thing Monday morning."

Even as Markus snarled under his breath, Declan replied, "If he can't make that, I'll let ye know." Then he disconnected the call. Arching a brow at him, his alpha stated, "Ye may have just lost yer job."

Markus scoffed as he turned his attention toward the open doorway. "I don't give a shit." To his surprise, his words were true. Then he voiced another belief. "I gotta funny feeling my mate is going to need us."

Declan tucked his phone into his breast pocket as he stood beside him, looking into the room where Lark was wrapping a brace around Ronan's left knee and leg. "We'll help yer mate," he assured softly. "Once we figure out what his problem is."

Sighing, Markus felt his ire ease to be replaced by relief. "Thank you, Alpha."

After a few slow nods, Declan frowned as he focused on Markus. "Is that accusation ye just made true?"

"What accusation?" Markus asked absently. His mind was already focused on the still human lying in the bed.

Alpha Declan rested his hand on Markus's shoulder, catching his attention. "Yer comment to Sheriff Parkinson about why he hasn't stepped down, yet?"

Markus grimaced as he nodded. He'd planned to tell his alpha, after all. "It is," he confirmed. "I overheard him a couple of weeks ago. I hadn't gotten around to telling you." Dipping his head in submission, Markus offered, "Sorry, Alpha. I should have found the time sooner."

"Aye, I wish ye would have, since this is affecting the pack," Alpha Declan replied, squeezing his neck lightly. "But I know now." Huffing a sigh, he grumbled, "Just another thing on my plate. Finding a way to roust him and have a hand in his replacement."

Markus nodded absently as his alpha released him, a speculative look on the bigger man's face as he started texting someone on his phone. Movement from within his spare bedroom coupled with the sound of Ronan's moan yanked his attention back to his mate. His human had turned his head, and his arms were sliding a little on the mattress, his fingers clenching and unclenching.

Unable to resist, Markus rushed into the room. He stopped at the side of the bed and grabbed one of Ronan's hands in both of his own. Staring down at the human Fate had made for him, he admired the big male before him.

After Ronan had passed out, Markus had slung the duffel bag from the tent as well as the rifle strap over his shoulders. Then he'd lifted his mate into his arms. Markus had hurried to his truck as swiftly as possible.

Once Markus had Ronan tucked safely into the passenger seat, he'd headed home. He'd called Alpha Declan on the way. Never had he been happier of the fact that Lark — the alpha's mate and a doctor — had retired from the hospital he'd been working at the prior year. Lark had set up a private practice, which primarily catered to the shifters in the pack, but the kind human would never turn away any patient.

Markus took a moment to admire his mate's nearly shaved dark hair and strong jaw. His wide shoulders and broad chest disappeared under the blanket Markus had spread over him, hiding the hint of love handles Markus had noticed in the shower. Instead of detracting from the human's appearance, Markus had thought it gave him character.

When Markus had removed the man's flannel-lined jeans, thick wool socks, and heavy boots, he'd noted how Ronan had certainly been prepared for the cold weather. His clothes might have been dirty and a little worn, but they were of excellent quality, telling Markus the man hadn't always lived in a tent in the woods. He'd tossed those clothes as well as the rest he'd found in the duffel bag into his washing machine, hoping that returning them clean to his mate would be seen as a peace offering for undressing him without permission.

He desperately wanted to know his human's story. Except, he needed him awake for that. He also needed him awake so he could actually ask permission to explore every bit of his human . . . and perhaps apologize, too.

While Markus had loved the earthy aroma of his mate, even laced with the undertones of sweat and dirt, he would bet his motorcycle that his mate would appreciate being clean. How he'd damn near shaved his head was a testament to that.

Squeezing Ronan's hand gently, Markus leaned close and crooned into his ear, "Come on, Ronan. Time to wake up." He peeled away one hand and cradled the man's skull, enjoying the scrape of the bristly hair felt against his palm. "Let me see those gorgeous brown eyes of yours, hmm?"

Ronan came awake like a shot. Yanking on Markus's clasped hand, he jerked him forward. His human used the momentum to haul Markus around like a ragdoll.

In an instant, Markus found himself lying on his back on the bed. Ronan lay sprawled over him, pressing his forearm against his throat, constricting his airway just a little. His dark gaze bored into him, distrust simmering in their depths.

"Who are you?" Ronan barked. "Where am I?"

Even as Ronan demanded answers, Markus could see the pain swimming in his eyes, too. His human was fighting it, but his body betrayed him. He needed rest and relaxation, a place to heal and perhaps regroup from whatever dogged his steps.

Markus had every intention of giving that to him . . . and more. "I'm Markus, remember?" he began. A flick of his gaze toward Declan told him his alpha had pulled Lark half behind him but still stood nearby in case Markus needed an assist. Meeting Ronan's burning gaze once more, Markus told him,

"You passed out from pain. I brought you to my home." After a heartbeat, he couldn't help but add, "You're totally safe here, Ronan."

Ronan stared hard at him with furrowed brows. His scent screamed of confusion and distrust. Finally, although he didn't relax the pressure on Markus's throat, he peered around the room.

When Ronan spotted Alpha Declan and Lark, he tensed further. "And them?"

"The big guy is Declan McIntire and his husband, Doctor Lark Trystan," Markus replied, swallowing to get moisture to his throat. Being manhandled by his mate in bed, even under such tense circumstances, caused Markus's prick to swell and his mouth to water. "I called the doc over to look at your leg. Of course Declan would come since you're a stranger."

"And possibly dangerous," Ronan mumbled, finally easing the pressure to Markus's throat. He rolled away from him — too bad — and pushed to a sitting position. Glancing down at himself, Ronan frowned as he bluntly asked, "Who washed me?"

Fighting to keep his embarrassment from heating his cheeks, Markus admitted, "I did." When Ronan's eyes narrowed, he quickly added, "I apologize for taking the liberty, but you were, well, dirty, and if Lark needed to work on your leg, it should be done while clean."

For a long moment, Ronan just stared at him.

It went on so long, Markus lost his fight with his flesh, and his cheeks heated, telling him he blushed. "I-I wanted to take care of you after hurting you. I'm sorry."

That seemed to be what Ronan had been waiting for. In a deep, gruff voice, he claimed, "For the record, I like briefs." Then he focused on Lark. "And the brace?"

"You have an awful lot of scar tissue in that area and a lot of swelling," Lark told him. "Whatever you've been doing has aggravated your injury. I recommend icing, heating, and elevation for at least a week." The doc grinned as he batted his eyelashes. "Unless you bond with Markus. Then maybe it'll only take a couple of days to subside."

Resting his right hand on the mattress beside his hip, Ronan eyed the brace. "Can't really sit around, doc," he muttered, frowning. He rubbed his other hand over the skin near the top of the brace as he lifted his gaze to meet the small human's. "What do I owe ya?" Just that fast, Ronan's expression clouded. "Not that I have a way to pay ya. Fuck."

Not liking the way Ronan rubbed his palms over his face or how his scent of frustration rolled from him, Markus couldn't stop himself from reaching for the man's hand. He took it and gently massaged it between his own. The move drew Ronan's attention, and when he stared at him with a mixture of shock and confusion, Markus squeezed his hand and smiled.

"You don't owe Lark anything," Markus told him. "You're going to be pack." He refused to think of any other outcome. "So it's on the pack account."

Ronan narrowed his eyes. Slipping out his tongue, he licked his lower lip, drawing Markus's attention to the full bit of flesh. His confusion intensified, obviously having caught Markus's attention.

After swallowing hard enough to cause his Adam's apple to bob, Ronan glanced from his hand, to Markus's face, to the alpha pair, then back to Markus. "What the hell is going on?" Scowling, he shook his head slowly. "Why the hell would you help me? What the hell is pack?" His eyes narrowed further, as if he were rerunning the conversation through his brain. "And bonding? What's that? Like getting married or something?" Markus didn't even have time to respond before Ronan continued, "I ain't marryin' anyone just for help." His voice lowered to a mumble as he finished, "Don't need to drag anyone else into this mess."

Markus did his best to ignore Ronan's immediate denial of marriage. That wasn't what bonding was anyway. Instead, he focused on what his human had revealed—that he was indeed in some kind of trouble.

"I'm about to tell you all kinds of unbelievable things, Ronan," Markus told his clearly confused and wary human. "All I ask is that you listen with an open mind." Watching as Ronan's eyes narrowed once more, he added, "After all, you must have had some experience in things not being what they seem in order to be on the run from . . . someone?"

Ronan's nostrils flared. "How do you know?" His gaze strayed to the uniform shirt Markus had thrown back on after their shower. "Fuck!" He yanked his hand so hard, Markus finally had no choice but to release it. "Did you run my ID or prints?" Scrambling toward the side of the bed, Ronan muttered in a pained tone, "I gotta get outta here."

"I didn't run anything!" Markus declared, but Ronan didn't seem to be listening. Instead, he was peering around the room, maybe looking for his pants. Knowing the desire between mates wasn't all on the paranormal side, Markus decided to use that physical contact to help distract Ronan from whatever he was thinking—and planning.

Markus once again grabbed for Ronan. Gripping his shoulder with one hand and his hip with the other, he yanked him back to the center of the bed. His shifter strength made it easy to force Ronan flat to his back.

With a quick turn of his own body, Markus sprawled over the man Fate deemed his, his knees bracketing his mate's thighs. He grabbed Ronan's wrists and pressed them to either side of the bed on the mattress. Seeing the larger man's surprised expression, Markus saw the move coming even before his human bucked beneath him.

Only Markus's increased strength allowed him to keep Ronan firmly in place.

"I didn't run your fingerprints," Markus told Ronan again. "Or your name. Hell, I don't even know what your full name is," he admitted. "I didn't look through your stuff."

Although, he'd been damn tempted.

"I wanted all that information to come from you," Markus admitted. "Once you trusted me."

A muscle jumped as Ronan clenched his jaw. "If I'm to trust you, why are you holding me down?" he asked through gritted teeth, all the while tugging lightly at his wrists.

Markus guessed it wasn't an attempt to pull free as much as it was his hope to gauge just how tight a grip he was using on him. Seeing as he had no intention of letting his mate go, ever, he kept his hold firm enough to keep him still, but not so hard as to hurt. In his hope to help the man relax, Markus even used his thumbs to massage the pulse points on each hand.

"So, to start, why don't I tell you something about us that you can never tell another soul?" Markus hoped getting the conversation started would help. *At least, it can't hurt.* "This is something you must take to your grave"—he couldn't help but wink as he continued—"which could be several hundred years from now. Welcome to the fountain of youth."

That definitely drew Ronan's attention. "What the hell are you talking about?"

Grinning widely, Markus purred, "Ah, got your attention now, huh?"

Unable to help himself, seeing as his mate's face was just so damn close, Markus dipped his head and pecked a kiss to his lips. He wished he could capture Ronan's lips fully, but he resisted the urge. Lifting his head again, he pinned a steady gaze on Ronan—who sported a shocked expression, once more.

Taking a deep breath—and a big chance—Markus told him, "I am a shifter. A wolf shifter. I can turn into the animal at will, and I have enhanced senses, like smell, hearing, and eyesight." As Ronan continued to gape at him, Markus had to smirk as he stated, "How do you think I tracked you down this morning? I rounded the camp and located your smell on the wind."

CHAPTER FOUR

Ronan knew he needed to snap his mouth shut. He really did. He even needed to tell the man lying over him that he was full of shit . . . or maybe to get the hell off of him. Ronan figured it really shouldn't be all that hard to force the man to release him, either.

Instead, he felt his body betray him . . . at the worst possible time. His cock thickened behind the thin fabric of his boxer-briefs. His blood heated faster than he could remember it doing in a decade. Even the hairs on his arms stood up in a way that didn't have anything to do with his sixth sense regarding when an enemy was near.

"I, uh . . . what?" Ronan felt his cheeks heat as he stumbled over his words. Scowling at the grinning man sprawled over him, he managed to gather a thought together and grumbled, "Get off me."

"Promise not to run," Markus countered.

With his knee in a brace coupled with not knowing where his clothes were, Ronan knew his compulsion to flee had been foolish. He'd just been running for so long. At this point, it was his default action.

That notion created a ball of shame to twist in his gut.

A marine who runs away from a fight. Pathetic.

Except, Ronan knew he didn't have the ability to fight the people after him.

"I promise not to run," Ronan told the man holding him down. "You'll send me on my way as soon as I answer a few of your questions, anyway."

Markus eased to Ronan's right, releasing his wrists. Reaching over him, he grabbed the blanket and yanked it back over his lower body. He didn't climb off the bed, however, sticking close to Ronan's side.

Ronan eased to a sitting position, uncertain what he thought of Markus's obvious advances. A quick roll in the sack would definitely relieve stress. If he answered a couple of questions for these men, maybe he could arrange it before they urged him to get moving.

As Ronan rested against the headboard, shoving a pillow behind him in the process, he glanced toward the large black man and his tiny blond husband. The doctor eyed Ronan with concern while his husband sported an inscrutable expression.

"I'm not ever going to send you away, Ronan," Markus claimed, redrawing his attention. "I'll get that through your thick skull eventually."

When Markus softened his words with a teasing smile and a wink, Ronan sighed. "You're offering me a place to lie low for a while?" With the dull throb radiating up his leg, that really did sound like heaven. "Why?" Recalling the weird shit Markus had spouted, Ronan smirked at the man. "Because you're crazy?"

Markus reached over and took his hand again. "Not crazy, but I've heard that's a human's initial reaction when we tell them about our kind."

Feeling Markus's calloused palm slide against his own caused Ronan's gut to clench a little. Butterflies bumped within him in a way he hadn't felt since . . . in longer than he cared to admit. His fingers curled instinctually, and he slid his digits between Markus's own, twining them.

What is it about this man that scrambles my brain so?

"Did the doc give me something?" Ronan asked, wondering if that was what was causing his confusing responses. "Is that why I'm having trouble focusing?"

"No, I didn't give you anything," Lark told him with a

shake of his head. "Do you need something?" he asked, stepping forward. "Are you in pain?"

Ronan quickly indicated no. "Just confused about—" He closed his mouth and took a deep breath. No way did he want to admit to some of what he was feeling.

"Relax, Ronan," Markus murmured. "Confusion is understandable." He squeezed Ronan's hand, adding, "I bet you've been through a lot recently. Do you want to tell us why you've been hiding in the woods?"

Sighing deeply, Ronan glanced around the group. If these guys believed they had the ability to change shape, maybe they would believe him. Of course, even if they did, there was very little they could do to help him.

Then I'll need to be on my way sooner rather than later. Oh, well. It can't be helped.

Ronan opened his mouth, but before he could get a word out, a thud sounded from beyond the door and a deep voice hollered, "Markus? You asshole." A man with light-brown hair, hazel eyes, and similar features to Markus skidded into the room, using the doorframe to slide around to a stop. Casting an accusing glare on Markus, he stated, "I just heard my brother found his mate from Beta Dixon. The beta!" He pointed at Markus. "Why didn't I hear the news from my own brother? I should have been the first person you called."

Markus rolled his eyes. "Stop being so dramatic, Ron." Turning to Ronan, he stated, "This is my brother, Ron Reussmin. He's a bit dramatic, but you'll get used to it."

"O-Okay." Ronan didn't know what else to say.

Turning back to Ron, Markus told him, "I would have called eventually, but Ronan needed medical attention."

Ron's expression morphed into worry as he peered at Ronan. "You okay, man? Anything you need, we're here for ya."

Ronan once again found himself at a loss for words. "Uh, thank you."

What rabbit hole have I fallen down?

"So." Ron clapped his hands together as he grinned at Declan. "Alpha Declan, did I miss the explanations? I could shift if you need someone to."

Markus growled from beside him. "If anyone is getting naked in front of my mate, it's me," he declared gruffly.

Ron rolled his eyes. "Don't be ridiculous," he stated, waving his hand dismissively. "If he freaks out, you need to be human so you can calm him."

Even as Markus opened his mouth, possibly to blast the man again, Ronan asked, "How can you guys really believe you, uh . . . change into an animal?" The very idea was completely ridiculous to him.

"'Cause it's true, Ronan," Ron claimed with a grin. "I'll show you." Then he whipped his shirt over his head.

Markus lifted his free hand and covered Ronan's eyes.

Ronan snorted as he grabbed Markus's wrist and pulled it down. "I was in the military, Markus," he told him. "I've seen plenty of naked men."

"Another military man," Ron quipped with a grin. "Sweet."

"Wait a moment before ye shift, Ron," Declan ordered, lifting one hand, palm out. "There are still a couple of things to explain before ye change."

Lark snorted. "Yeah. Let's try not to freak out your brother's mate, huh?" Then he smiled at Ronan. "Okay, first thing to keep in mind is that when a shifter is in his or her animal form, they are completely cognizant. They still know who they are and can think and reason while in their animal form."

Frowning, Ronan tried to process everything these strangers were sharing. In truth, he thought they were all nuts. Still, they seemed so certain of what they were telling him.

Nodding slowly, Ronan muttered, "Seeing is believing."

"That is very true," Markus agreed. Rubbing his thumb over the back of Ronan's hand, he told him, "We just want you to be prepared for what you see. Even while in wolf form, none of us would ever hurt you."

Ronan glanced around at everyone, seeing their nods. "You all believe you're . . . wolf shifters?" Just saying the words out loud sounded ludicrous.

Lark lifted his hand, grinning. "Not me. I'm human."

"The rest of us, yes," Declan told him with an understanding smile. "And just as ye said, seeing is believing." He focused on Ron. "Go ahead and shift."

Ron grinned brightly, then moved off to the side near the foot of the bed. Turning his back on them, he kicked off his boots, then bent and pulled off his socks. He peered over his shoulder, still sporting a large smile.

"Remember, I would never hurt you," Ron reminded Ronan. "You're my brother's mate, and I'll know that even as a wolf."

Then Ron slid his jeans partway down his hips before crouching on the floor.

Glancing away from the mostly nude male, Ronan met Markus's gaze. "Your mate? What does that mean?"

"To me, you are a gift from Fate," Markus claimed solemnly. "The other half of my soul."

"I—"

Ronan didn't know what he would have said to that, but an odd popping sound interrupted him. Grateful for the interruption, he peered toward the noise. He blinked once, twice, certain what he was seeing would change.

It didn't.

Ron's body was reshaping, his limbs were cracking and adjusting shape, and his skull reformed. Then a tail sprouted as fur grew. Right before Ronan's eyes, Ron truly shifted into a light-brown wolf, remarkably similar in color to his hair.

"Oh, fuck me," Ronan whispered as the animal shook out its fur, then promptly turned and sat, staring at him.

The wolf's tongue lolled from its mouth, and it was . . . wagging its tail. Even the glitter in the animal's eyes made it appear to be laughing at him . . . or maybe full of mischief.

"Oh, I plan to fuck you as soon as you'll let me," Markus rumbled into his ear, yanking his attention from the wolf.

"What?" Ronan mumbled inanely. His mind began to swim a little, and he swayed on the bed. Rubbing his hand over his face, he tried to focus. "How is this possible?"

"I've wondered that a time or two myself," Lark admitted quietly. "It's one of those things that, well, it just is."

Ronan took a few deep breaths as he looked first at the wolf, then at the looks on the men's faces. Lark's smile was full of understanding, as if he'd been exactly where Ronan was and knew what he was going through. If he was human as he claimed, and he was married to a wolf shifter, it made sense that he did.

Declan stared at Ronan intently, as if waiting for him to freak out or pass out.

The expression Markus sported concerned Ronan the most. There was so much hope gleaming in his eyes. The man obviously wanted him to accept everything they were telling and showing him.

Considering the strangeness of it, Ronan realized that meant Markus expected him to stick around.

There's just one huge problem with that.

"I'm wanted by the military police," Ronan blurted out. "If my name pops up anywhere around here, these mountains will be crawling with the military."

"Well, we certainly don't want that," Declan drawled, a smirk curving his lips. "What the hell did ye do?"

The man's first comment didn't surprise Ronan. He'd expected it. The fact that he asked what he did, *did* surprise him. Ronan had half expected the guy to tell him to move on. It was obvious that Declan was the boss, even if Ronan hadn't noticed Ron call him the alpha.

After seeing Markus's brother turn into a wolf, the title made sense.

"I busted my brother out of a military hospital," Ronan told everyone. "They were refusing to allow anyone in the family to visit, claiming it was at his request, but I know my brother." He couldn't help but growl as he recalled the situation he'd discovered his brother in. "He would *never* stop our mom from going to see him, no matter the injury."

"Oh, good grief," Lark mumbled, crossing his arms over his chest. "I know where this is going." His blue eyes sparkled with the intensity of the anger in his expression. "Were they running illegal experiments on him?"

Ronan shrugged, confusion filling him upon hearing the doctor's ire . . . and his question. "I don't really understand what the experiments were supposed to do," he admitted, scowling at the blanket covering his lap. He hated thinking about Bailey lying so still and pale in that bed. "I couldn't make heads or tails of the shit on his charts, so I snuck Bailey out of there and took him to Brian. Bailey is still there, as far as I know."

"Who's Brian?" Markus asked softly, rubbing his hand over Ronan's stomach. "Another brother?" Then his brows furrowed. "How would you know if you've been hiding out in the woods for . . . how long?"

"Corporal Brian Haas," Ronan explained, glancing around at everyone. "My career as a marine ended when an IED exploded, tearing apart the ligaments in and around my knee. That was late into my third tour. Brian was a medic on my team."

Nodding, Markus slid his hand down and twined their fingers. "Okay. So you swiped your brother from a military medical facility and left him in your friend's care?"

Ronan nodded. "Exactly." Refocusing on the doctor, he added, "I took pictures of Bailey's charts as well as a few other patients. I gave copies of the information to Brian. As far as I know, Bailey hasn't regained consciousness, and Brian hasn't been able to figure out why." Grimacing, he told them, "The MPs are after me because they think I have Bailey. I'm wanted for kidnapping and theft of government property."

"And how long ago was that?" Markus asked again.

"Almost nine months ago." Ronan grimaced. "And my brother is still in a coma, not that Brian has been able to figure out why."

Just saying that caused Ronan's gut to churn. Those bastards had done something to his baby brother, and he didn't know what.

"Well, then." Declan's grin turned predatory. "We're going to need detailed information on where the facility is, how ye entered, and how ye secreted yer brother away."

"And I'd like to look at the chart information of the patients," Lark told him. "I can check to see if it's something we've seen before with the other facilities we've shut down."

Ronan's eyes widened as he glanced between them. "Wait. What?" Had he heard that right? "You've shut down . . . medical facilities?"

Declan's expression hardened as his gray eyes narrowed. "We've stopped scientists from kidnapping our kind, running experiments on them, then using their findings to augment their own soldiers."

Lark huffed a deep sigh from where he was tucked securely against Declan's side. "It seems every time we stop one group, another one pops up."

With his mind reeling at that revelation, Ronan struggled to latch onto, well, anything. These men—shifters—believed him. They'd dealt with these issues before. They'd stopped others.

Finally, Markus's soothing touch, the way he rubbed across his abdominals with the hand that wasn't holding his own, registered.

Turning to focus on Markus, Ronan saw the other man's concerned gaze.

"We will help you," Markus vowed. "You and your brother."

"Why?" Ronan whispered the word. While he had so many questions, that was the only thing that seemed to make it to his mouth. "Why help me?"

"You're my mate, Ronan," Markus told him. His hazel eyes were flooded with warmth as he stared at him. "Your problems are my problems. Your family, my family."

Could it really be as simple as that?

"So, you believe I'm the other half of your soul," Ronan began slowly, trying to process everything he'd just learned. "And because of that, other members of your pack will help me . . . what? Hide?"

"Die, actually."

Upon hearing a deep voice Ronan didn't recognize, he snapped his gaze toward the bedroom's doorway. He spotted a fair-skinned, broad-shouldered man leaning against the frame. His thickly muscled arms were crossed over his chest, and he stared at Ronan with glittering, pale-blue eyes.

"What?" Ronan tensed as the urge to flee once more surged through him. "Die?"

"Way to make friends, Dixon," Declan stated, his tone teasing. A smile toyed around the corners of his lips as he returned his attention back to Ronan. "This is Beta Dixon Holsteen, my beta, and what he means is, we'll create a fake trail to some undecided location, then fake yer death."

Frowning, Ronan muttered, "What about my family?"

CHAPTER FIVE

M arkus felt his gut churn. "Your family? You have a family?"

He hadn't considered that.

Unable to help himself, Markus tightened his hold on Ronan's twined fingers. "A wife? Kids?" After a second, he blurted out, "Husband?"

Ronan stared at Markus as if he had two heads . . . but only for a couple of heartbeats. Then he shook his head. "No. I mean my brother, my sister, my parents," he explained. "My parents and sister are already mourning the fact that Bailey is injured and ordered no visitors before succumbing to a coma. How can I make them believe I'm dead as well?"

Sighing with relief, Markus closed his eyes for a brief second. "I see."

"Hmmm, there's a possibility of letting yer family know ye're in hiding, uh, witness protection," Declan mused slowly, clearly choosing his words carefully. Rubbing his chin with the hand not clutching Lark's waist, he murmured, "I don't know if the bad guys would leave them alone if they found that out, though."

"And if the reason your brother is stuck in a coma is something we can reverse, we would be returning him to your family," Lark pointed out. "We won't stop until it's fixed."

"So, to accept your help," Ronan stated slowly. "I have to accept that I'll never be able to see my family again."

Markus scented Ronan's distress, and the smell caused his gut to twist uncomfortably. His instinct screamed at him to please his mate, to make him happy. Unfortunately, Markus didn't know a way to do that.

"We could bring them out here," Beta Dixon muttered, although he sounded uncertain.

Declan arched a black brow. "Yer reasoning and plan?"

Wincing, Dixon shook his head. "Preliminary ideas only, Alpha," he admitted. Glancing Ronan's way, he added, "But pleasing our mate is always at the forefront of a shifter's mind. It needs to be taken into account." His lips curved into a wry smile as he added, "If for no other reason than to keep Markus's mate from doing something stupid."

Ronan's eyes narrowed while the spicy aroma of annoyance filled the air. "I'm a damn marine. I don't do stupid."

Dixon grinned widely as he lifted his hands in placation. His blue eyes danced, betraying his mirth. "Everyone does dumb shit if their family is in trouble." Just that fast, Dixon muttered, "When they're adults who think for themselves, anyway."

Markus was so damn tempted to ask his beta what he meant by that, but he resisted. That had more to do with the fact that Declan began speaking.

"I agree with ye, Dixon," Declan stated. "Plus, if we need to bring Bailey here for treatment, it would make sense to bring the whole family." Rubbing his jaw, he softly added, "We just need to come up with a viable cover story."

"Cover story?" Ron cocked his head. At least he'd pulled his jeans on at some point after shifting back to human form. "What kind of cover story?"

"The kind we can tell a family who can only learn part of the truth," Lark supplied with a smile, a mischievous twinkle lighting his eyes. "And I have just the idea."

Declan scoffed. "I'm almost afraid to ask, my mate."

Lark stared wide-eyed at Declan, his look one of complete innocence. "What? How can you say that?"

Dipping his head, Declan pecked a kiss to Lark's lips. "Because I know the way yer devious mind occasionally works."

Beaming a grin Declan's way, Lark quipped, "That's the nicest compliment you've given me in quite a while."

"Do ye mean since this morning in the shower when I—"

Lark slapped a hand over Declan's mouth as his cheeks took on a pinkish hue. "You've spent way too much time with Jared," he grumbled, clearly embarrassed.

Gripping Lark's wrist, Declan pulled his mate's hand away from his mouth. While rubbing the human's pulse point, he murmured, "Sorry, my love. He gets bored while Kajika is overseeing the construction of their new house." After pecking his lips, Declan added, "And his name is Prier now."

Rolling his eyes, Lark snorted. "Of course."

Markus knew that Declan and Lark were referring to their head enforcer and his mate. For the last twenty-seven years, their pack's head enforcer had been known as Carson Angeni. He'd met his mate, Jared Templeton, over a decade before. A couple of years before, they'd used an attack on their home to fake their deaths.

After traveling for a while, Carson and Jared had returned to their pack lands. Over the next decade, they would lie low and build new identities. The pack was slowly getting used to calling them Kajika and Prier Bozeman.

"Well, I'm all kinds of curious," Beta Dixon commented, amusement in his tone. "What's your plan, Lark?"

"Easy. We meet up with Ronan's family and explain how Bailey was attacked by an experimental weapon developed by the government," Lark told them with a grin. "If he survives, he has to go underground along with Ronan. They can choose to join them." Suddenly, Lark frowned as he touched a forefinger to his upper lip. "Um, I guess I should ask how old your sister is. Is she in a relationship?" Growling softly, he muttered, "What if she doesn't want to give up her life? I didn't think of that. I—"

"My sister's name is Isabel," Ronan cut in. "And she's fourteen, so she better not have a damn boyfriend."

"Or girlfriend?" Ron pointed out, clearly teasing.

Ronan rolled his eyes. "Or girlfriend, although at least then she couldn't end up pregnant."

Dixon snorted as he shook his head. "Well, it sounds like we have a lot to sort out." Focusing on Declan, he stated, "But first, I thought I'd let you know that Cliff located that missing hiker. Poor sap was wearing sandals and slipped off a soft trail. He ended up twisting his ankle so he couldn't climb back up again," he finished with a derisive snort, clearly expressing his opinion of the man's choices.

"May the gods save us from morons," Declan grumbled. "Thank ye for the update." Clearing his expression, he focused on Ronan. "So, Ronan, ye have a lot of explaining to do."

Lark nodded. "Tell us everything."

Almost an hour later, Markus ushered everyone out of his house. He closed the front door, then rested his back against it. Tipping his head back, he blew out a long, slow breath.
Finally.

Markus heard the creak of furniture, returning his attention to his mate who waited in his upstairs spare bedroom. Pushing away from the door, he hurried to the kitchen. He grabbed an icepack from the freezer and a hand towel, then rushed back upstairs.

Arriving back in the bedroom, wrapping the towel around the icepack as Markus moved, he spotted Ronan swinging his legs over the side of the bed.

"Whoa, where do you think you're going?" Markus demanded, crossing to him. He rested his hand on his mate's shoulder, keeping him from rising. "You're in no position to go anywhere."

Ronan's cheeks took on a slightly pinkish hue. Pointing to the backpack in the corner, he claimed, "I was just gonna see about finding some clean pants."

Shaking his head, Markus revealed, "I put your clothes in the washing machine. You didn't really have anything, um, clean." Hoping to keep Ronan's focus away from the liberties he'd taken, he urged his mate back onto the bed. "Lie back down and get comfortable. I brought an icepack. Doc's orders, remember?"

Even as Ronan growled a little under his breath, he allowed Markus to help him back to the middle of the mattress. "Thought you said you didn't go through my stuff."

Shrugging while propping the icepack against the swollen area of Ronan's knee, Markus corrected, "I told you I didn't run your identification. I didn't go through your wallet." He pointed at the backpack. "I even didn't go through your front pouch with the pens and other shit, although the flash drive you had me pull out of there and give to Declan made me damn curious. I didn't think washing dirty clothes was being intrusive."

With narrowed eyes, Ronan grabbed the blanket and pulled it back over his waist and upper thighs. "And the pockets?"

Unable to help himself, Markus teased, "You make it a habit of leaving stuff in the pockets of your dirty clothes?"

"I know I had a handful of bullets in the jeans I was wearing," Ronan told him. "Along with a few twists of twine and a lighter."

"Always prepared to light a fire, huh?" Markus replied knowingly. At the same time, he pointed toward the dresser. "Everything I found is in that blue candy dish up there."

Ronan looked like he wanted to rise to his feet and check. Instead, he repositioned the icepack Markus had placed against his leg. At the same time, he muttered, "Thank you."

"You're welcome," Markus replied softly, then fell silent. He struggled with what to say next. He desperately wanted to climb into bed with his mate and ask all about him, but his sexy human's furrowed brows and closed expression made him hesitate. Finally, Markus came up with, "Are you hungry? When was the last time you ate?"

Lifting his chin, Ronan met his gaze. "I could eat," he replied softly. "I had oatmeal and bacon over the fire this morning."

Smiling, Markus commented, "You can never go wrong with bacon."

A small smile curved Ronan's lips. "Hell, yeah," he murmured.

"Are you allergic to anything?" Markus pressed as he took a step backward, his mind running through what he had in his fridge and pantry.

Ronan shook his head. "No. Cast iron stomach here."

Markus grinned. "Good to know." After a few seconds of hesitation, where Ronan just stared back at him, he returned to the side of the bed. "I can't resist."

When Ronan arched one brow, Markus didn't say more. He cradled his mate's jaw in a light hold as he placed his other on the mattress for balance. Bending at the waist, he held Ronan's gaze as he brought their faces together.

Pleased that Ronan didn't pull or turn away, Markus sealed his lips over the human's. He licked lightly at his bottom lip, asking for entrance. To Markus's delight, his mate opened to him.

Tipping his head to the side a little, Markus fitted their mouths together more firmly. He teased his tongue along Ronan's appendage before swirling it within his mate, tasting and mapping his human. Markus relished the chance to learn Ronan and enjoyed how his mate wasn't a passive kisser, his tongue coming out to play before pushing into Markus's mouth.

When Markus found himself fighting his desire to climb onto the bed and take the kiss further, he instead brought it to an end.

Easing back, Markus panted softly as he stared at Ronan. "Damn," he whispered. "I sure could get used to that in a hurry."

Ronan cleared his throat, his Adam's apple bobbing. "Yeah. We'll talk about that while we eat, huh?"

Markus nodded. "Deal."

Then he hurried from the room. He'd just reached the main floor when he heard the unmistakable sound of tires on gravel. Wondering if his alpha or Lark had forgotten something, he headed toward the front of the house.

Peeking out the window, Markus groaned. "What the hell is she doing here?"

As Markus watched, Martha parked her *Suburban* and climbed out. She closed her door, then opened the one behind it. From within, Martha withdrew a large paper sack.

Markus turned away from the window, thinking quickly. Taking the stairs two at a time, he yanked off his uniform shirt as well as his undershirt in one go. Pausing in the doorway of the room where Ronan rested, Markus marveled in the fact that he had his mate in his home.

"What's up?" Ronan asked, his gaze roving over Markus's bare torso. There was appreciation in his human's eyes as well as a hint of confusion.

"An unexpected visitor just pulled up," Markus told him. "I'll try to get rid of her as swiftly as possible."

"Her?" Ronan questioned, the hint of jealousy in his tone pleasing Markus. "Someone from your pack?"

Markus shook his head. "A woman from town who's asked me out a few times," he admitted. He wasn't going to hide anything from his mate, even the uncomfortable stuff. "I've always turned her down."

The doorbell rang through the house.

"I'll explain more soon," Markus assured before heading to his own bedroom.

As much as he'd wanted to place Ronan right in there first thing, he thought that might have been a little forward.

"You better be getting a shirt."

Upon hearing Ronan's yell, Markus grinned. "I am," he called back as he stuffed his shirts into a backpack he pulled from his closet's top shelf.

"Why the fuck do I even care?"

Markus's sharp shifter hearing allowed him to make out Ronan's grumbled words. Shaking his head, he knew his mate was still struggling to accept. He also knew that, in time, he would. Even the humans in the pairing felt the pull to be with their paranormal.

As Markus pulled on a t-shirt, he heard the doorbell sound again. He shoved a couple more shirts into the bag, making it appear filled out. Then he hustled back through the house, dropping it on a chair in the front room in clear view of the foyer.

Yanking open the door, Markus snapped, "Yeah?" He pretended to appear surprised upon seeing Martha there. "Uh, hey, Miss Martha," he greeted. "I'm real sorry, but now's not the best time."

"I heard you were headed out of town for some kind of family emergency," Martha stated with a beaming smile as she held up the bag. "And I don't want you to go on an empty stomach, so I brought you some things."

As Markus wondered who at the station had gossiped about his family, Martha pressed forward. Good manners and a bit of wariness caused him to step backward, keeping space between them.

Martha spotted the bag on the chair, and she smiled. "I'm

so glad I caught you in time, Markus." She once again took a step toward him. "I bet you weren't even going to take anything. Then you'd have to buy something from one of those unhealthy chain restaurants."

To Markus's surprise, Martha rested a hand on his chest, which made his skin crawl even as she smiled sweetly up at him.

"You really need someone to take care of you, Markus," she told him, a hint of feminine persuasion in her tone. "As soon as I heard about your family emergency, I knew you'd need some support. I grabbed a couple of bear claws from my bakery as well as some sandwiches and things from Darrell's Deli. I even grabbed a change of clothes from home," she revealed, shocking Markus even further. "I'll come with you."

Gaping, Markus had no idea what to say to that.

What the hell?

Chapter Six

R onan couldn't believe he was doing this. He hardly knew the man. Surely he could send some lady he had turned down on her way.

Except, Ronan always listened to his gut, and his stomach told him to get down there and stake his claim.

He'd always listened to his gut.

It was easier said than done, however, because he still only wore a pair of underwear. At least knowing some woman was dropping in on his handsome host caused his boner to wilt. The kiss had been damn hot.

Shoving off the blanket, Ronan eased off the bed. He grimaced as he took a few steps, but between the brace and a few hours rest, his knee didn't feel too bad. Heading in the direction Markus had gone in to change, Ronan easily found his bedroom.

Ronan would have felt bad raiding the man's drawers for a pair of sweatpants, but seeing as Markus had stripped him down, washed him, then tossed all his clothes in the washer, he didn't. They were pretty close in height, even though Ronan was a bit broader than Markus, so he guessed the sweats would fit okay. He quickly pulled the fabric over the brace, grimacing as he wiggled it up his leg a bit, before allowing them to rest low on his hips.

Then Ronan made his way to the stairs. He arrived at the top just in time to hear the woman tell Markus that she planned to go with him. Ronan didn't know where she thought he was going, but he'd noticed the backpack the other man had carried when he'd passed his door after changing.

As a marine, Ronan had needed to think on his feet many, many times. He was happy to play on that.

Limping down the stairs, Ronan announced his presence by saying, "Hey, babe. Sorry, I'm not much help packing." He gripped the handrail tightly and bit back a wince as the throb in his knee intensified. "Let me toss a couple of sandwiches together while you finish packing. That's easy enough."

"Shit, Ro. You shouldn't be out of bed." Markus rushed up the stairs to him. He wrapped an arm around his waist while gripping Ronan's upper arm with his other hand. "What the hell are you thinking?" Then Markus tipped his head close and whispered, "Babe?"

Ronan smirked at him. Keeping his voice equally low, he mumbled, "Ro?" In all his forty-seven years, he'd never had anyone give him a pet name. He kind of liked it.

"Who is this?" The woman had moved to the bottom of the stairs, and she stared up at him with narrowed brown eyes.

As Markus began helping Ronan down the stairs, he told her, "Miss Martha, this is my boyfriend, Ronan Diego."

Ronan didn't know where Markus had pulled the surname from, but he went with it. "Ma'am, nice to meet you." Seeing as he used his hand to grip the railing tightly, he dipped his chin in greeting instead.

As they reached the bottom of the stairs, Martha backed up a couple of steps. "You're gay?" she gasped, lifting her empty hand to her lips. The hand holding a large, white paper sack was pressed to her stomach, just under her breasts. The shock was written all over her flushed cheeks. "But you never hinted at . . . my friends said . . . ."

As Markus guided Ronan toward a sofa in the huge space that acted as a living, family, and front room all rolled into one, he told her, "Well, Miss Martha, I've never flaunted it, but I've never denied it, either. It really just never came up."

Markus shrugged, his smile wry. "Never found a guy I wanted to take out on dates before now." Then Markus turned his attention on Ronan. "Relax here, Ro." He winked. "Don't worry about food. Miss Martha brought us somethin'."

"Oh." Ronan relaxed on the sofa, his back toward the corner. As he stretched his left leg along the sofa cushions, he offered, "Thank you, ma'am. That was awful kind of ya."

"Y-You're welcome." Martha placed the bag of items on the chair next to Markus's bag. "Um, where did you meet? How long have you been dating?"

Ronan had to give her credit. She was clearly trying, so she must not have had a problem with homosexuals. Of course, he had no clue how to answer either of those questions since he didn't know the area.

Markus grabbed a throw blanket from off the back of the sofa as he answered. "We met in Colorado Springs six months ago." He smiled down at him as he wrapped the fabric around his shoulders. Leaving one hand there, Markus claimed, "Ronan's in private security, so when he injured his knee on the job, I told him to come out here to recover."

Slipping one hand from under the blanket, Ronan placed it over Markus's on his shoulder. "Long-distance relationships are hard."

Still smiling, Markus nodded. "This was supposed to give us some time to see if we fit while in each others' space."

Squeezing Markus's hand, Ronan took a guess at something he'd overheard Martha saying and commented, "But now I can be here for you."

"Yeah," Markus murmured.

Markus began to bend, his focus on Ronan's lips. He realized the man was going to kiss him right then and there . . . in front of Martha. Obviously, the guy had no qualms about showing affection.

Ronan had never been in a relationship, so it had never come up. It took every bit of self-control to keep from tensing.

"Well, I'm so very pleased you have someone to see you through this," Martha stated, causing Markus to straighten back up. She smiled as she headed toward the front door. "Please offer my deepest well wishes to your family." She grabbed the doorknob and started through the still-open door. "And to Ron, too."

That sounded like an afterthought, but neither of them called her out on it.

"Thank you, Miss Martha," Markus called instead. "I appreciate your kindness."

Then she shut the door.

A few seconds later, the roar of an engine told Ronan that the woman was leaving. He tipped his head back, resting it against the sofa. Smirking, he arched one brow.

"In demand, are you?" Ronan teased.

Markus shrugged, his voice coming out dry as he stated, "She's a widow of three years, and she's just started feeling okay to date again." He grimaced as he admitted, "Trying to let her down easy was hard, but she's not my mate, so what was the point?"

Ronan pondered that. "So, this mate thing. That's why I felt the need to come down here and . . . stake my claim?"

While Markus moved to the chair and picked up the sack, he nodded. "Yeah. Humans feel it, too."

"So we don't really get a choice?" Ronan didn't know if he liked that idea—some mystical hoodoo messing with his senses.

Markus placed the sack on the sofa next to Ronan's knee. "It's not really like that," he countered. "Let me get your ice-pack and some drinks first. Then I'll explain."

Ronan nodded. "Fair enough." As soon as he opened the paper sack, the sweet scent of some baked good reached his nose, and his stomach rumbled appreciatively. "Oh, dang," Ronan muttered. "That smells fantastic."

Touching his shoulder before heading upstairs, Markus called, "Probably her blueberry bear claws. She knows I have a weakness for them."

Peering inside the bag, Ronan confirmed Markus's guess. He pulled out napkins first, then spotted two pastries wrapped in the parchment paper-like sleeves favored by bakeries. Ronan eased them out and placed them on the napkins.

"Yup," Ronan murmured, licking his lips. Unable to help himself, he picked up one, peeled back some of the paper, and took a big bite. The sugary goodness burst across his taste buds, and he moaned softly. "Oh, damn," Ronan mumbled around the bite. "So good."

Markus chuckled as he trotted back down the stairs, holding the icepack and hand towel. "Been a while since you had one of those?" he teased. As Ronan nodded in confirmation, Markus used the hand towel to prop the icepack into position. Meeting Ronan's gaze, heat filling his hazel eyes, Markus stated, "The sounds you're making are damn near pornographic. I can't wait to hear them for a completely different reason."

As Ronan's blood heated thinking about another reason to make those noises, he watched Markus head to the kitchen. The main floor had an open concept, allowing him to watch the man's ass as he moved. The high and tight cheeks called for him to squeeze and massage them.

When Markus moved behind the bar, obstructing his view, Ronan snapped his attention back to the bear claw. He wrapped up the rest and placed it on the napkin while trying to get his thoughts and body under control. Never in his memory could he recall reacting so viscerally to a man.

Am I okay with this?

Ronan pulled out the sandwiches that had been below them. According to the labels on them, one was a roast beef with cheddar cheese and the second was turkey and swiss. Both sounded fantastic to him.

Calling out the choices, Ronan asked Markus which one he would prefer. "Both are fine by me," he added before pulling out the last items. "There's also a couple of bags of apple slices."

Markus appeared at his shoulder. "I'd love the beef and cheddar, but if that's your preference, you can have it." While he spoke, he grabbed the coffee table and dragged it the couple of feet necessary to bring it close to the sofa. "Beer, water, or orange juice?"

Spotting the containers in Markus's hands before he placed them on the coffee table, Ronan cocked his head. "Is that freshly squeezed?" he asked curiously, since the orange drink was in a pale-blue water container.

"Sure is," Markus confirmed. "I have a couple of orange trees in my greenhouse."

Handing over the beef and cheddar, Ronan took the juice. "I just want a couple of sips," he admitted, popping the cap. "It's been months since I've been able to have fresh juice." Before the container reached his lips, Ronan paused. "Uh, unless you don't want me drinking straight from your container?"

Markus's lips curved into a lascivious leer as his hazel eyes darkened. "Oh, Ronan. We've already made out a few times. I don't think swapping spit is an issue."

Ronan accepted that and took a couple of swigs of the juice. The bitter-sweet fluid burst across his taste buds. He rolled it across his tongue, relishing the slight bite before swallowing. Then Ronan drank some more.

"Oh, that's good," Ronan commented as he closed the cap on the container. "Thanks." Then he pointed at the beer. "Unless I'm on meds I don't know about?"

While Ronan recalled asking earlier, he figured it didn't hurt to double-check.

"You're not," Markus confirmed, popping the cap on the glass bottle and handing it over. "So, you talked about not having a choice," he started slowly as he unwrapped his sandwich. Holding Ronan's gaze, Markus told him softly, "Yes, there is always a choice, but I'm hoping to convince you of how good we'd be together."

Ronan chewed the bite of sandwich he'd taken before saying, "You don't know me. How can you be sure we'd be good together?"

"We would have been attracted to each other anyway," Markus claimed. "Fate just gives us that extra burst of desire needed to push aside some of our natural inhibitions."

"Natural inhibitions?" Ronan frowned. Before taking another bite, he asked, "Like what?"

Smiling, Markus teased, "Well, the fact that I'm a cop, and you're on the run." He winked. "You stopped and listened anyway."

Ronan hummed around his bite of food. "Okay," he muttered before swallowing. "Why would you want to saddle yourself with a middle-aged, ex-soldier who comes with a shitload of problems?" he asked bluntly before taking a swig of his beer.

The bitter brew flowed across his tongue, a little darker and hoppier than he preferred. Checking the label, Ronan realized it boasted some micro-brewery from the area. Taking a second drink, he decided he didn't mind it. Besides, a guest didn't complain about the food and drink.

"Not a fan?" Markus asked perceptively. "They have other flavors, but that's all I had left on hand."

Shrugging, Ronan admitted, "I like 'em a bit lighter. Got plenty of shit for it from a few of the guys on my team."

Markus chuckled. "We'll go there, and you can do some sampling." Then he told him, "And it's been said that Fate brings mates together when one or both of them need each other most." Smiling at Ronan, Markus told him, "And a mate is a blessing, a gift, a person who can complement each other. She doesn't make mistakes."

Ronan pinned a narrow-eyed gaze on Markus. "You really believe that?"

Nodding once, Markus confirmed, "I really do."

"Huh."

They fell into silence for a few minutes as they ate. Markus seemed to know that Ronan needed time to process his words. After all, it was a lot to take in.

Except, is it really?

Ronan thought about everything. He was in the home of a wolf shifter. The man's buddies were going to help him with his brother, his family, and the military. He was damn attracted to the guy sitting across from him.

When will I ever get another chance at something that could be so damn good? The man claims to want to devote his life to me.

Ronan wasn't an idiot. He knew a good thing when it fell in his lap. His life had been in turmoil, living one day to the next.

Could I really take that leap of faith?

Meeting Markus's gaze, Ronan asked, "So, how do you claim your mate? I heard something about bonding, I think."

Markus froze, an apple slice halfway to his lips. "Uh, sex," he answered bluntly. Lowering the hand with the food in it to his thigh, he pointed at Ronan's neck with the other. "And I bite you, giving you a claiming scar to bond us."

"Bite me?" Ronan rubbed his neck, unease slithering through him.

That sounds painful.

Once again, Markus seemed to be able to read his mind. "Oh, it only hurts for a split second. I promise," he claimed. His eyes narrowed as heat once again filled them. "Then, you'll orgasm from the pleasure of it."

Ronan gaped at the handsome blond. "Seriously?"

Holding his gaze, Markus nodded once. "Seriously."

While Ronan figured he might be doing this for all the wrong reasons, the blood surging to his cock made it difficult to think. He hadn't had sex in years. Outside of the few remaining members of his team, he couldn't count on anyone. Bonding with this man—this shifter—would change all of that.

"Okay."

Markus straightened, his brows shooting to his hairline. "Okay?"

Ronan wrapped up the last couple of bites of his sandwich and placed it back in the bag. "Yeah." He eased to a standing position and held out his hand, palm up. "Okay."

For a couple of seconds, Markus stared at him in disbelief. Then the man moved faster than Ronan could follow.

CHAPTER SEVEN

M arkus had no idea why Ronan had accepted so quickly, and he vowed to find out eventually, but right then, he didn't care. His mate had accepted, and that was enough for him.

Leaping to his feet, Markus ignored Ronan's hand. Instead, he swept him into his arms.

"What the—" Ronan began.

Rushing up the stairs, Markus told him, "Relax. I got you."

"You can't possibly—" he began again.

Markus had already reached the second floor. With a laugh, and skipping the spare room, he headed to the master. "How do you think you ended up here to begin with?" he teased.

"Uh, guess I didn't think about it."

Laying Ronan in the middle of his king-sized bed, Markus peered down at him. Seeing his mate in his bed, sprawled out and looking amused, a fresh surge of desire coursed through him. His human stood an inch taller than himself, was bigger and broader, and he couldn't wait to explore every inch of the ex-military man.

"You're looking at me like you want to eat me," Ronan commented with a wry smile. He moved his hands behind his head, his bulging arms flexing deliciously. "So go ahead."

Groaning upon being given permission to do whatever he wanted to his mate, Markus hardly knew where to start.

"Naked," Markus decided, reaching for the drawstring of the sweats Ronan wore. "Gonna get you naked."

When Ronan lifted his hips to assist him, he winced and moved his hands down to either side of his hips, catching his weight.

Right. Injured. Get with it.

"I'm sorry, Ronan," Markus crooned, rubbing his hands over his sides and abdominals soothingly. "Just relax. I'll take care of everything."

"I'm not an invalid, you know," Ronan grumbled, frowning.

Markus shook his head as he eased the sweats down Ronan's body, revealing his black boxer-briefs as well as the black brace on his left leg.

"I don't think you're an invalid," Markus countered, returning his focus to Ronan's face. He teased his fingertips along the top of the brace. "But you are injured, and I don't want to do anything to make it worse."

"The only way you could make it worse was if you didn't do something about this." Ronan waved his left hand to indicate the erection tenting his underwear. His voice turned grumbling as he added, "Can't remember the last time I've been so turned on. What the fuck is up with that?"

Markus whipped his shirt over his head, then started on his jeans. As he undressed, he admitted, "When mates meet, our arousal ramps up, increasing our libido and helping us push past those insecurities and inhibitions I was telling you about." As Markus bent to untie his boots, he added, "And don't worry. I'll take damn good care of that."

A moment later, Markus stood naked before his mate. He reveled in the appreciative gleam filling Ronan's deep brown eyes. His lips were curved into a hungry smile, and he blatantly rubbed his erection through his boxer-briefs. He'd once more moved his other hand behind his head.

As Ronan swept his gaze over Markus's form, he dipped his fingertips beneath the band of his briefs and tipped them down, revealing his swollen crown. "You go commando," he commented as he rubbed over his leaking head. "That'll make fucking you whenever I want much, much easier."

Markus's asshole clenched as he climbed onto the bed. "You're welcome to my ass any time you want," he promised, reaching out to join Ronan in teasing his crown. The soft skin of his head was already slick with pre-cum. "But right now . . ." Markus brought his fingers to his mouth and licked the fluid from them, pulling a moan from his throat. "Right now, I'm going to fuck you and make you mine."

Needing confirmation one more time, Markus asked huskily, "You ready for that, Ronan?"

Ronan nodded. "I'm ready."

Wasting no more time, Markus gripped Ronan's underwear. He eased them down and off, tossing them over the side of the bed. Then he draped himself over his mate's strong, broad body, bracketing his thighs with his knees.

When Markus pressed his erection against Ronan's, both men groaned. He rocked his hips, rutting lightly against the other man. He slid his hand behind his mate's neck, gripping it, urging him to turn his head a smidge.

As soon as Ronan followed his urging, Markus sealed his mouth over his mate's. He delved his tongue past his lips, licking and tasting. His mate's natural flavor burst across his taste buds combined with the food and drink they'd been enjoying.

Groaning softly, Markus reveled in the delicious flavors. He rutted harder, his body flaming as his balls pulled tight. His need fired through his veins, coupling with the feel of his mate beneath him and the sound of the grunts and groans Ronan was feeding him, sending his senses soaring.

Markus felt his balls begin to tighten, and he realized just how close to orgasm he actually was. Except, when he tried to pull away, he found himself held tight in the strong bands of Ronan's arms. His mate gripped his ass with one hand and his neck with the other, not allowing him to put any space between them.

Groaning roughly, Markus turned his head to the side, breaking the kiss. He sucked in a much-needed lungful of air, only to let it out as he groaned Ronan's name.

"Fuck, yeah," Ronan snarled into his ear. "Love the sounds you make. Fucking come all over me."

With another moan, Markus obeyed. He pressed his forehead into Ronan's shoulder as a full-body shudder worked through him. Zings of blissful fire coursed through his body as his balls pumped his cum through his dick. With each jolt of ecstasy, Markus marked his mate's abdomen with his seed . . . his scent . . . filling his wolf with satisfaction.

Ronan growled roughly into his ear as a shiver worked through the body below Markus. The heady scent of seed not his own flooded the room. His mate whispered his name on a sigh as his grip tightened, then loosened.

A low rumbling chuckle escaped Ronan. "Fuck, man," he mumbled before sighing again, his arms relaxing a bit more, although he didn't release Markus. "Can't remember the last time I busted a nut from kissin' and frottin'. Fuck!"

Easing his own hold on Ronan's neck, Markus pushed onto his elbows. He grinned down at his mate, taking in his blissful expression and flushed face. His kiss-swollen lips were curved into a satisfied smile.

"It's only gonna get better," Markus claimed softly. "That's just to take the edge off."

Ronan hummed as he shook his head. "I'm almost fifty, babe." His tone turned chagrined, and he shrugged. "I don't think I can get it up again for a while. Sorry. I just couldn't seem to stop myself once we got going. Felt too good."

Markus winked. "Well, I'll be happy to prove you wrong, then."

Pushing onto his hands and knees, Markus silently lamented the loss of Ronan's strong arms around him as he let him go.

"If you still want my ass, feel free," Ronan told him, relaxing on the bed. "But I don't think my pecker will do much. Really."

"Remember when I told you about that ramped-up sex drive?"

Ronan nodded, his brows furrowing.

"Well," Markus drawled as he reached over and pulled open a nightstand drawer. "It's not just the paranormal that's affected." Once he found his bottle of lube, Markus pulled back and winked at his human. "It's both of us. Fate's way of pushing us together a little."

"She sounds like a bossy bitch," Ronan commented with a smirk.

Markus nodded as he eased backward so he could kneel between his mate's calves. "You're right about that." Rubbing up and down his good leg, he found his focus drawn to Ronan's semi-hard prick and the white cream coating his abdominals. "I'll get you cleaned up."

As Ronan nodded, Markus dipped his body and opened his mouth. He heard his mate's harsh inhale and peered up at him through his lashes. His forever love stared at him with shock on his face as he registered how Markus intended to clean him.

"You okay?" Markus asked softly as he began lapping at their combined cream. He recognized his own slight tang mixed with Ronan's heavier flavor. Humming, he took another swipe.

"Uh, shouldn't you ask if I'm clean first?" Ronan rumbled even as the muscles of his abdominals fluttered under his tongue.

That brought Markus up short. "Are you ill?" Rubbing

over Ronan's chest, he swirled his fingertip around one nipple. "As a shifter, I can't get or give any diseases, but if you're ill, we'll let Lark know so we can monitor it."

Ronan's eyes widened as he shook his head. "No, I'm not sick." As if a lightbulb clicked, he added, "You intend to bareback me."

"I do," Markus confirmed. With a wink, he added, "Just like you'll be doing the same to me."

As Markus returned to cleaning Ronan with his tongue, he grinned, hearing his mate's groan. As he searched out every trace of seed on his human's skin, he popped open the tube of lubricant. Using his other hand, Markus gently urged Ronan's legs wider, giving him greater access to his most intimate parts.

By the time Markus had finished cleaning Ronan's prick, his mate was almost at full mast again. "Told you," he crooned as he rubbed his cheek over his shaft. "Gonna make you fly tonight."

As Markus moved his lips to Ronan's balls, lapping at them gently, he poured a liberal dollop of lube onto his fingers. He used his thumb to shut it before dropping it to the mattress. Finally, he suckled one of Ronan's balls into his mouth as he massaged his man's opening, testing his tension level.

Ronan groaned softly as he shivered beneath him. "Y-You already have," he mumbled, spreading his legs even wider. "Damn, you were right. Impossible."

Markus eased his finger deep into Ronan as he released the ball from his mouth. "Paranormal," he whispered before blowing warm air over Ronan's damp flesh.

Responding by groaning and arching his body, Ronan pressed into his ministrations.

Giving his mate what he obviously needed, Markus eased his finger out, then slipped a second one in. He felt his human clamp onto him and heard his breath catch. To distract him, he licked a line up his erection before gently sucking on his frenulum.

"O-Oh, shit," Ronan mumbled. "Markus."

Markus smiled against Ronan's flesh. Continuing to tease his lover's cock and balls with his lips, teeth, and tongue, he worked his fingers in and out. The delicious scent of Ronan's arousal flooded his nostrils, causing his own need to flood his body, and he knew he didn't have long before he lost control.

As soon as Markus slipped a third digit into Ronan's chute, his lover threaded his fingers through his hair. His mate tugged gently and growled.

"Now," Ronan demanded. "I'm not gonna break. Fucking take me already."

"Never thought you would," Markus countered, even as he eased his fingers out and pushed them back in. He did it once more as he crawled up his mate's body. "I can't put you on your knees," he murmured. "Would you prefer on your side?"

Markus had felt how tight his mate was, so he would bet it had been a while since his big, powerful mate had been on the receiving end, and he wanted to make it as painless as possible.

Ronan met his gaze with dilated eyes. His cheeks were flushed, and his chest rose and fell in harsh panting breaths.

"If you can shove a pillow under my ass, I'd appreciate it," Ronan told him. "Then get up here."

Taking Ronan at his word, Markus eased onto his knees. He grabbed a pillow as he pulled his fingers free from Ronan's channel. Gripping his mate's ass cheek, he lifted the man and pushed the pillow beneath him, changing his angle.

Markus grabbed the lube and poured some onto his dick. As he spread it over his shaft, he groaned at the sensation.

"Come here," Ronan ordered again, lifting his arms and beckoning to him.

Sliding forward, Markus guided his erection to Ronan's hole. He teased his tip against his opening, testing his muscles. To his surprise—and pleasure—Ronan's muscles gave way, opening right up for him.

Groaning, Markus pushed forward a bit more, sinking into the blissful heat of his human's body.

"Yeah, that's it," Ronan rumbled, grabbing Markus's upper arms. "Take my ass, wolf."

Unable to do anything but obey, Markus thrust harder, sinking all the way to the root. He dropped his body on top of Ronan's, groaning at the ecstasy of feeling his mate wrapped around him for the first time. His body shuddered as sensations shot through his groin.

Ronan threaded his fingers through Markus's hair, tugging lightly to gain his attention.

Markus met Ronan's gaze and spotted the lust and pleasure lighting the man's brown eyes.

"Fuck me, babe," Ronan urged, rocking his hips to grind his ass against Markus's groin. "I know you're desperate to."

His mate was right.

With a groan, Markus eased his cock nearly all the way out of Ronan. He immediately shoved back into the other man. As his hips slapped against Ronan's cheeks, he couldn't resist doing it again . . . and again . . . and again.

"Yeah, that's it, Markus," Ronan rumbled into his ear. "Fuck, that feels good. You like it when I squeeze ya?"

As Ronan spoke, he did exactly that. He tightened his chute muscles around Markus's length each time he withdrew.

Markus growled as his nerve endings lit up. Every move his mate made, from the ripple of his chute muscles to the way he held him in a tight hold with his arms and good leg, caused blissful fire to erupt within him. His balls pulled tight once more, but he fought against it.

Wanting Ronan to come with him, Markus adjusted his angle. It took him one, two more strokes until he felt the jolt travel through his mate's body. He zeroed in on that spot, pegging Ronan's prostate with each rut.

"There it is," Markus muttered into Ronan's ear. "Let go and come, my mate. Coat my skin once more."

Ronan panted harshly in his ear. "N-Not sure I-I can."

Markus lifted his head enough to meet Ronan's gaze. Never slowing his thrusts, he purred, "You can do it, my mate. Come for me. Don't fight it. Just relax into the tingles in your balls."

His lips parting, Ronan sucked in harsh gasps. After three more ruts, his leg dropped from Markus's waist. A deep noise that sounded torn from Ronan's throat filled the room.

Feeling the sweet pressure tighten around his cock, scenting the exquisite aroma of Ronan's cum, Markus reveled in knowing he'd pleased his mate. His own senses flew as his orgasm crashed through him, pouring his seed into his mate.

When Markus's canines lengthened and his instinct to bite flooded him, he didn't fight it. He sank his teeth deep into his mate's flesh, marking him inside and out.

CHAPTER EIGHT

Forcing open his eyelids, Ronan had to blink several times to get his eyes to focus. He struggled to remember why he felt so groggy. Being on the run, he always needed to be on guard.

So what the hell happened?

Then Ronan registered the heavy arm slung around his waist, the leg between his own, and the heat all along his backside. Not only that, but there was a distinctive ache in his ass.

Holy shit. What the fuck?

"Relax, Ronan." The arm around him rubbed over his chest. "We don't need to meet up with the others for a couple of hours, yet."

Hearing the sleep-roughened tenor, it all came rushing back.

Markus finding me. Taking me home with him. Wolf shifters. Their willingness to help.

Ronan relaxed as he blew out a deep breath. Releasing the tension that had flooded him with his confusion, he pressed into the man behind him. He recalled their frotting, then fucking.

Then that bite.

"Holy fucking shit," Ronan mumbled, allowing his eyelids to slide back closed. "Did you seriously get me off three times?"

When Markus chuckled softly behind him, his warm breath fanned over Ronan's neck, causing the hairs to stir. The

sensation trickled down his chest. His nipples beaded pleas-
antly, and even his morning wood twitched.

"Told you my bite would make you come," Markus murmured against his skin. Then he licked over the flesh where
his neck met his shoulder.

Sparks shot through him, and Ronan sucked in a sharp
breath as the tingles settled in his balls.

"What the hell was that?" he hissed.

"This is where I bit you," Markus told him before licking at
him again. "It will always be sensitive to my touch. You like?"

Markus licked that place again, creating more tendrils of
pleasure to fire through his veins.

Gritting his teeth, Ronan grabbed Markus's wrist. "Stop
that or move your hand south, Markus," he ordered, pushing.

Chuckling softly, Markus did as he'd been told. He
skimmed his palm down Ronan's chest, over his abdominals,
then gripped his shaft. "Rock into my hand, Ro," Markus encouraged, tightening his grip. "Take what you need."

Then Markus sucked on the pleasure-giving spot on his
neck.

Ronan groaned as he gave himself over to the other man's
stimulation. He rocked his hips, thrusting into his grip. Grabbing Markus's hip behind him, he pushed into his groin,
pleased to feel the other man's answering erection. Then
Markus wedged his arm underneath his body, curled it
around his torso, and plucked at his nipple.

In far shorter a time than Ronan could have possibly imag-
ined, he lost himself to the stimulation. His balls pulled tight,
and his gut clenched. He groaned roughly as his orgasm
surged through him.

As Ronan came back to himself, he sluggishly tried to find
his tongue. He wanted to offer to return the favor. Ronan had
never considered himself a selfish lover.

"*Now* it's a good morning," Markus mumbled softly.

That was when Ronan realized Markus was using the sheet to gently swipe at his back.

"Did you come, too?" Ronan couldn't help but ask.

Markus hummed. "I did. Pleasuring you, hearing your cries, smelling your seed. So fucking sexy."

Ronan ignored the continued dampness and rolled to his back. Grabbing Markus, he hauled the man close. He paused just a second so he could say, "I want a morning kiss, but I don't remember brushing my teeth last night."

"You didn't," Markus told him with a grin. "But I don't mind."

Then Markus pressed his lips to Ronan's. He kept the kiss light and didn't delve into his mouth, but Ronan didn't care. After several more pecks, Markus relaxed, resting his head against Ronan's chest.

"How are you feeling?" Markus asked softly after several minutes of silence.

Ronan gave that question the respect it was due and thought about it for a moment. "A little overwhelmed," he decided on. When Markus began to lift away from him, Ronan tightened his hold. "But there's nothing wrong with that. A lot has happened in the last twenty-four hours."

Damn. Is that all it's been?

Still draped over him, Markus rubbed his cheek against Ronan's chest as he nodded. "That's understandable," he murmured. "Just know this, I've been waiting for you for a long time. I'm dedicated to making this work."

"Even if you have to quit your job?" Ronan asked, because he just couldn't see how he could be in an open relationship with a cop when he was a wanted man.

"Even then," Markus replied, surprising him. Chuckling softly, he rubbed over Ronan's abdominals soothingly. "I've been in that position for almost fourteen years, although most of it was part time. People have started noticing that I'm not aging. It's about time I take a step back and make everyone think that I moved away." Tilting his head back, Markus met Ronan's gaze. "I'm pretty self-sufficient out here, so we wouldn't have to go into town for any reason. Anything that we do need, our pack-members can get for us."

Ronan smiled down at Markus. "You a survivalist, too, Markus?"

"Too?" Markus arched a brow in curiosity.

Chuckling, Ronan revealed, "Why do you think I've been able to disappear off the grid for almost nine months? Between the skills I learned as a marine, and the training I went through after getting back, plus stocking up the staples just in case of catastrophe, I know how to live off the land. It's not surprising that it was a bunch of paranormals that found me."

"Well, I never really considered myself one, but yeah." Markus chuckled softly. "I guess you could say that most paranormals are survivalists of one sort or other."

"You mentioned a greenhouse and making your own orange juice," Ronan pointed out. "Got any farm animals?"

Markus nodded. "A small herd of goats for milk. Chickens for eggs. A few cows and a bull."

Ronan laughed, grinning broadly. "You're a bigger survivalist than I am." Then he sobered. "Unless you're running off the city power grid."

"Uh, yeah. Some of the time," Markus told him. "I'm not totally self-sufficient."

Lifting his head, Ronan pressed a kiss to his forehead. "We'll fix that."

Markus peered up at him with hope in his eyes. "Then you're okay with staying here?"

Damn. Am I?

"Yeah," Ronan admitted. "Yeah, I am." Turning and peering out the window at the early-morning, pre-dawn light, he told him, "I have a house in Idaho, but it's just a place to hang my hat." Ronan dipped his chin and refocused on Markus. "My family is an hour from there, but I can't go back there.

Not really."

"And we're going to try to convince your family to come here," Markus reminded him.

Ronan nodded, hoping convincing them wouldn't be too difficult.

"You're forty-seven, right?" Markus asked suddenly.

Ronan nodded again. "Yeah."

"And your sister is fourteen?"

Smirking, Ronan realized what Markus was getting at. "Huge spread, right?"

Scoffing, Markus nodded. "Yeah."

"I was a contraceptive mishap when my mom was sixteen," Ronan admitted.

"Oh, shit!" Markus squeaked. "Really?"

"Mmm-hmm." Ronan threaded his fingers through Markus's hair, finding the motion soothing. "My father's parents were super supportive and understanding. My mother's parents disowned her." Grimacing, Ronan grumbled, "I could never understand how parents could act that way toward their children."

"Well, damn," Markus muttered. "That sucks. I'm sorry."

Ronan shook his head. "Don't apologize," he countered. "The grandparents I did know were fantastic. They got married, moved into the basement of their house, and my grandparents helped support them and raise me." Smiling, Ronan recalled all the fond memories he'd had of his father's parents. "My grandfather was in the military. I chose to follow in his footsteps."

"And your brother? Bailey?" Markus asked curiously. "How old is he?"

"He's thirty-seven," Ronan told him. "My parents had him when I was ten." Grimacing, he admitted, "He followed me into the military."

"And your sister?"

Ronan realized Markus was like a dog with a bone, trying to understand.

Or a wolf with a bone.

Chuckling softly at that thought, Ronan told him, "Another accident. My father had a vasectomy, but they had unprotected sex a little too soon for it to have fully taken affect."

"Oops."

Nodding, Ronan silently agreed. "They love us all, regardless of how we came about."

"How'd they take it when you came out to them?"

Ronan winced as he remembered the first year or two. "I didn't tell them until I'd been in the military for a couple of years, so they wondered if some officer had raped me or something." Scowling, he growled, "Not true. It took them a while to accept." He knew he needed to prepare his . . . partner, mate . . . whatever. Ronan held Markus's gaze as he admitted, "I've never brought anyone home to meet them, so there could be some . . . resistance at first."

"I'll handle it as long as you're by my side," Markus stated, peering at him steadily.

Nodding once, Ronan replied. "Okay." Then he added, "My brother is bi, not that he's bothered telling them. I don't know about my sister." Scowling, he grumbled, "Hopefully, she hasn't discovered sex, yet."

"At fourteen, eh." Markus waggled his hand back and forth. "Got a fifty, fifty shot, I suppose."

Ronan groaned. "Ugh. Why did you have to tell me that?"

Markus just chuckled.

Grumbling under his breath, Ronan left it alone. "Hey," he murmured, once again peering at Markus. "You said you have animals, right?"

"I did."

"Did you care for them last night?" Concern filled him.

Grinning, Markus winked. "It was tough pulling myself away from you after you passed out from pleasure, but yeah.

I took care of them."

Relaxing, Ronan stated, "Oh, good."

"I used the sweats you'd borrowed and shoved my feet into my boots," Markus explained. "As a shifter, we have a higher tolerance to cold, but let me tell you, you weren't the only reason I hurried through chores."

Rumbling a soft laugh, Ronan tried to imagine that. "I'll be getting fully dressed to help, thanks."

Markus laughed, too, even as he warned, "But not until Lark gives the okay." Then he lifted his head and peered toward the nightstand. Groaning softly, he tightened his hold for a few seconds before releasing it.

"Speaking of the animals, it's about time I get a move on," Markus told him. With an eyebrow waggle, he asked, "Care to take a shower with me? I'll wash your back."

"I've never washed another guy's back before," Ronan admitted. In the military, he'd always made it a point never to be too close or look too long at another. Still—"Yeah. I'd like to try that."

"Glad to hear it." Markus pushed the covers away and slipped from the bed. Holding out his hand, palm up, he urged, "Come on, stud. The day is starting."

Ronan took Markus's hand and allowed the man to help him from the bed. After so many months of sleeping in a sleeping bag on the ground, he sure appreciated the change.

So does my back.

Forty-five minutes later, Ronan limped around the kitchen. His lover had tried to get him to sit and relax, but that wasn't who he was—doctor's orders or not. Instead, while Markus was busy outside with the animals, he chose to start breakfast.

Ronan found the bacon and eggs as well as the hash-browns. After getting cheese out of the fridge, too, he realized he didn't see any bread, although the man did have a toaster. Deciding to ask about that later, Ronan began whipping up something tasty.

While the bacon simmered in a pan, Ronan grated the cheese. He also found some onions and green peppers, so he diced up some of those, too. When he was able to remove the bacon, he tossed the veggies into the pan to fry in the hot grease.

When the potato cubes were nearly browned, Ronan melted butter into another skillet. He noticed the butter was in a quart canning jar and wondered if Markus made his own from either cow or goat milk. The milk in the fridge was in a glass bottle, too.

"And he doesn't call himself a survivalist," Ronan murmured to himself, smirking.

After placing the eggs in the heated pan, Ronan stared out the window over the kitchen sink. The view was of the back yard. He spotted Markus tossing hay to the herd of goats and grinned. The man really was sexy, moving confidently between his creatures.

Markus turned and headed to the chicken coop. The man must have spotted Ronan watching, for he waved.

Smiling a little, Ronan waved back.

"Is this really what my life could become?" Ronan didn't know how the wolf shifters could accomplish it, but for the first time since he realized what was going on, he had hope.

CHAPTER NINE

"Stop the vehicles here, Kade," Ronan ordered, leaning forward from the center seat of the SUV several of them were piled into.

Enforcer Kade drove with Beta Dixon in the passenger seat. Alpha Declan and Lark were in the rear seat. Markus sat beside his mate, Ronan, in the middle.

Behind them, Enforcers Manon and Gracen drove a van, which was decked out with medical equipment. It would be safe to transport Bailey in it, assuming they could find Ronan's friend. They were in the middle of nowhere.

Kade obeyed, glancing around the forest. "Soooo, your buddy, Brian, lives way out here?"

"He does," Ronan confirmed. Grimacing, he admitted, "He's not just a survivalist. He's a doomsday prepper. He's sure the world will implode at any minute."

"Well, if it's remote enough to keep yer brother safe . . ." Declan mused, understanding in his tone.

"Exactly," Ronan agreed. "Plus, eccentric or not, he's the only doctor I was willing to trust." As he spoke, he pushed his door open. With his hands in view, Ronan slid from the vehicle. Moving a few steps away, he looked around as he called, "Corporal Brian Haas, I know you can see me right now." He glanced toward the vehicle. For just an instant, he met Markus's gaze before refocusing on the forest terrain around them. "I'm going to come forward alone. These guys are here to help my brother. I need to explain."

Markus growled low in his throat, not liking that idea at

all. "No wonder he didn't tell me about this when we decided to come here first."

"Bummer," Kade muttered.

As they watched, Ronan slowly limped forward. Dressed in camo pants and a black, long-sleeved Henley, he also still wore the brace Lark had fitted him with. His boots crunched on the frost-covered ground.

Ronan had just reached a tree fifteen feet in front of the SUV when a man stepped from the trees immediately to his right. He sported a thick dark beard, a strong frame, and stood an inch or so taller than his lover. Seeing as his mate didn't react, Markus figured his lover had known the man would be there. The guy carried a weapon, which he trained on their vehicle.

"What's the name of the little redhead I met at the bar in Cairo?"

The man was whispering, but Markus still heard the question anyway.

"Hameed," Ronan replied softly. "And he was a brunet."

The man stared at Ronan for a long minute. Then a slight smile curved his lips as he shoved the handgun into the holster on his thigh. "It's good to see you, Ronan. How come you didn't tell me you were coming?"

Ronan held out his hand, and the other man took it. "Hi, Brian," he greeted. They leaned in for a quick one-armed, back-slapping man-hug. "Your mainline is being monitored."

"What?" Brian growled softly. "No fucking way. I just checked it this morning."

"I've been assured that it is," Ronan replied with a shrug. "I'll have the guy who discovered it explain it to you so you can double-check his work."

"Hell, yeah, I want to double-check his work," Brian claimed. "Is he in that SUV with you?" Then his eyes narrowed. "What are you doing here, anyway? I don't have an update on your brother."

"I know you don't," Ronan replied. "I found someone who may be able to help, so I was hoping you'd come with us, and we'd collaborate." As if to sweeten the deal, Ronan added, "The hacker who figured out your shit is hiding in their woods, too."

Brian returned his hand to the butt of his weapon. "Who? Who's in those vehicles, Ronan?"

Ronan sighed deeply. "They're guys who have shut down facilities similar to the one I found my brother in," he told his friend. "There's a doctor, and a life flight medic, and their van is equipped to move Bailey." Lifting his hand, palm out, Ronan admitted, "I'm going to try to convince my family to go into hiding with me until these guys get it sorted out."

Brian stared at him for a long moment, his dark brows furrowed and a wary gleam in his dark eyes. "You trust these guys?" he asked softly.

Nodding once, Ronan admitted, "They've shown me things that . . . well, let's just say, they have secrets, too, and they have just as much reason to stop the guys doing experiments as we do."

The flash drive that Ronan had handed off to Lark and Declan had held a wealth of information. Lark had worked with several pack scientists and found, while the experiments weren't exactly the same as the ones being performed by the group they'd shut down a few years prior, there had definitely been similarities. Someone had been trying to get Bailey's body to accept some kind of serum to make him stronger, faster, and give his body advanced healing.

Prier and his buddy, Raul, had located the facility. They were in the process of hacking into their systems so they could figure out a way in. Unfortunately, the way Ronan had entered and exited had been corrected.

"Come with me, Brian," Ronan encouraged. "I promise on

my brother's life, they're safe."

Brian nodded slowly. "Okay. I'll meet you at the house."

"Thank you." Ronan fist-bumped Brian before beginning to limp back to the SUV. After he'd climbed in, he grabbed Markus's hand. "Thank you for trusting me. My buddy's paranoid."

"Ya think?" Dixon quipped.

Kade chuckled.

Markus squeezed Ronan's hand, saying, "You didn't give me much of a choice."

Grimacing, Ronan admitted, "You all talked about your shifter instincts to keep me safe." He glanced around at those in the vehicle before meeting Markus's gaze once more. "I feared you wouldn't allow me to go alone, and I had to. Otherwise, we'd never be allowed on Brian's property."

Bringing Ronan's hand to his lips, Markus kissed his knuckles lightly. "Our relationship is still new," he conceded. "We'll learn to trust each other in time."

After all, two days together wasn't enough time to truly get to know each other, bonded or not.

"Thank you." Ronan tugged their hands to his own mouth. Flipping their twined fingers, he nipped at Markus's pulse point under his wrist.

Markus smiled. After all, how could he not?

When Kade brought their vehicle roaring back to life, Markus returned his focus to what was going on outside. Brian was on a dirt bike, leading them along the overgrown dirt track. The branches closed in around them, scraping along the SUV's sides.

Declan groaned. "Please tell me those scratches are going to buff out."

Grunting, Kade shook his head. "Couldn't say until I get a closer look." The wolf shifter was one of the pack's mechanics.

Markus heard Declan sigh deeply behind him.

After several minutes of creeping along the grass and dirt

path, a small clearing opened before them. Brian pointed toward the left even as he branched to the right. He stopped his dirt bike before a shed and swung off.

"Go around back of that shack on the left," Ronan urged when Kade hesitated. "Trust me."

Kade nodded and did as he'd been bidden.

"Turn around and park," Ronan told him. "We'll have Manon back up to the shack."

"He lives in the shack?" Kade asked curiously.

Ronan chuckled as he shook his head. "No, Brian lives under it. He has a couple of different entrances, but the shack holds an elevator. It's how I took Bailey inside."

"Impressive," Dixon commented.

After Kade parked and shut off the SUV, they all piled out. Ronan did a quick introduction as Lark crossed to the trailing van and explained where to park. Then everyone met at the shack.

Brian pressed a knot in the wood, unlocking a small door. He swung it open, revealing a numerical pad. After he'd entered an access code, he pressed his thumb into a groove near the bottom.

A soft hum filled the air for a few seconds, then the doors opened revealing a metal freight elevator.

Closing the access panel, Brian led the way aboard. Once they were all closed inside, he punched in another code. The cage started descending.

Feeling boxed in, Markus shifted his weight from foot to foot. He scented the unease from several of the other shifters, and he knew he wasn't the only one who felt the same way. Taking an elevator into the earth felt way too much like getting into a cage.

"Relax, Markus," Ronan rumbled, wrapping his arm around his shoulders. "You're fine."

Markus wasn't certain what had tipped off Ronan, but he

appreciated the comfort. He pressed into his mate's side. That was when he noticed Declan had his arms around his own mate and was nuzzling and snuffling at his hair. Markus bet he was taking in his scent to keep calm.

"Everything okay, gents?" Brian asked, glancing around at them all. "A few of you claustrophobic or something?"

"Or something," Dixon replied before pulling a toothpick from his pocket and slipping it between his lips.

Brian opened his mouth, then spotted how Ronan was holding Markus, and his mouth snapped shut. His left eyebrow arched high, disappearing beneath his bushy, dark hair. "Somethin' you wanna tell me, Major?"

Ronan smirked as he replied, "This is Markus Reussmin, and I'm moving in with him."

For an instant, Brian stared at them in obvious shock. Then the soft thud of the elevator hitting bottom jerked him out of his stupor. As Brian and Dixon opened the doors, he glanced over his shoulder at them a few times.

As Brian led the way out, he asked, "You sure that's wise? With your problems and all?"

"We'll make it work," Markus stated, unwilling to allow anyone, even a friend of Ronan's, to try to undermine their relationship. "He's it for me, and I'm it for him."

Brian lifted a hand in placation as he shrugged. "Sorry." Then he turned and headed left. "So, you're the doc, right?" He peered at Lark.

Lark nodded. "Doctor Lark Trystan." He flicked a finger in Manon's direction. "Manon is the life flight pilot and a paramedic."

"And Ronan has shared my reports with you?" Brian pressed.

"He has," Lark confirmed.

"Well, I've just noticed a new development yesterday. I'm monitoring it, and it seems to come and go, but I don't know what's causing it or how to treat it."

"What is it?" Lark asked, concern and curiosity filling his voice.

Brian sighed deeply as he entered a code and led the way into a room. Most followed except Kade, Dixon, and Gracen. Those three hung out in the doorway.

Inside, a man who looked remarkably similar to Ronan lay still in the bed, although his body didn't contain nearly as much bulk. There were a number of wires attached to him as well as a couple of IVs. His features were pale, and his skin appeared clammy.

"This." Brian pointed.

Markus stared at a patch of reddish-brown skin on Bailey's upper right arm that appeared to be covered in . . . fur.

Crossing the room, Lark rested a hand on the blanket and leaned close. He hesitated just an instant before running his fingertips over the fur. In the next instant, it disappeared, giving way to smooth, pale flesh.

Markus scented Ronan's unease even before his mate asked, "Doc?"

Lark exchanged a look with Manon, then Declan. Finally, he asked Brian, "Can I take a quick look at his charts?"

Nodding, Brian grabbed a clipboard from off a nearby dresser.

The only sound was the crinkle of paper as Lark flipped through the pages. He paused, backed up a page, then checked the next one again. Moving to Manon's side, Lark pointed at whatever he was looking at.

Manon's tanned features paled. "Oh, fuck."

"You see it, too?" Lark asked quietly. "You really think?"

Nodding once, Manon muttered, "Gods, I hope we're wrong."

"What?" Ronan obviously couldn't keep quiet. "What do you see? Is he dying?"

Lark faced Ronan. He opened his mouth, closed it again, then sighed deeply. "I need to get him to a scientist friend of ours. Drake Whitton. He's seen this before and . . . he was able to help. If what I suspect isn't what it is, then he'd be able to help with that, too."

"Lark, are they really trying to create us again?" Declan asked gruffly.

Spreading his arms, a helpless expression crossed Lark's face. "I'm not sure. Lyle was a mistake, remember?"

"What's going on?" Ronan demanded. "What's your guess?"

Manon blew out a breath before saying, "There is one man on this planet who was born human but is now a shifter. Detective Lyle Sullivan was experimented on. His DNA was fucked with." Rubbing the back of his neck, Manon focused on Bailey. "But he didn't get . . . fur."

"Wait a minute." Ronan stepped forward, his fists clenching at his sides. "Are you saying . . . are you saying that those assholes at the facility are trying to make . . . you guys?" He waved his hand to indicate the others.

"That was *not* wolf fur," Lark declared. "It felt more like feline, but it's been a long, long time since I petted Grady's tiger. I'm just not sure."

"Hold it." Brian lifted both hands as he peered around at everyone. "What the hell are you all talking about? Shifters? Fur?" He focused on Ronan. "What the fuck is going on?"

Ronan rubbed his hands over his face, clearly at a loss for words.

Dixon smirked from where he leaned against the doorframe. After pulling the toothpick from his mouth, he rumbled, "Welcome to Oz, Dorothy."

"Wait, wait, wait." Kade waved his hand and shook his head. "We've always used the Alice and rabbit hole reference. What happened?"

Shrugging one massive shoulder, Dixon grinned widely. "Just trying something different. That's all."

While Kade grumbled under his breath, Ronan rested his hand on Bailey's sock-clad foot. "Can you help him, Doc?" He glanced between Lark and Manon. "You said this Drake guy helped someone named Lyle?"

Lark nodded. "If it's similar, yeah." Then his expression turned determined. "Even if it's something else, we'll do everything in our power to help him."

"Thanks, Doc," Ronan muttered, then allowed himself to be tugged back to Markus's side.

"Holy shit." Brian barked a laugh. "Paranormals are real," he crowed. "I fucking knew it!" Then Brian must have realized what he'd said, for his jaw sagged open. With a whispered, "They're real," his eyes rolled to the back of his head, and he began to drop.

Manon grabbed Brian before he could smack his head on the dresser.

Declan sighed. "Does anyone know if the same codes will take us out of here?"

CHAPTER TEN

Ronan felt Markus rest his hand on his thigh and realized he was bouncing his leg . . . again. Inhaling deeply, he let it out just as slowly. He rested his hand over Markus's and squeezed gently.

"Try to relax," Markus urged, rubbing his fingertips over the inseam of Ronan's jeans. "I have faith in the people of my pack. They'll help your brother."

Realizing Markus misunderstood what had him so nervous, Ronan tried to find the words.

Ronan had known his brother's health was out of his hands long ago. Bailey could have gotten hit by a car at any point in his life. In the military, he could have caught a bullet from an enemy, been struck by friendly fire, or even contracted some damn desert illness.

One way or another, Ronan couldn't control what happened to Bailey. Of course, having him infected by scientists doing research on shifter DNA had certainly never crossed his mind. Still, he knew his lover's friends would do everything within their power to help Bailey.

"That's not what I'm worried about," Ronan admitted. Squeezing Markus's hand, he forced a smile as he admitted, "I can't believe I'm beyond nervous to introduce a boyfriend to my parents for the first time."

Markus turned his hand over and threaded their fingers together. "We'll get through this together."

"I know." Then Ronan pointed at the split-level house on the right. "That's my parents' home."

Nodding, Dixon pointed at the sedan with deeply tinted windows to the left. "And that's someone watching your parents' place." He kept driving. After turning the corner, Dixon glanced in the rearview mirror. "That should mean your parents are home, though."

Ronan nodded as he glanced at the time on the dashboard. "They should be about ready to sit down to dinner."

"Let's sneak in through the back, then," Gracen stated, looking at a map of the neighborhood. "Like with many older homes, the plots are larger, and there are plenty of well-developed trees." Peering over his shoulder at them, Gracen smirked. "You grew up in this neighborhood. Know any ways to sneak in and out of your home?"

Snorting, Ronan shook his head. "Actually, no. Bailey was the one who pulled that shit . . . or so I heard." He sobered. "I joined the military right out of high school, so I was gone by the time he went through his teens."

"You must have still had a great relationship if he followed you into the military," Markus pointed out.

Ronan smiled sadly as he nodded. "Yeah. He wrote a lot, and I wrote back. I made sure I saw them as often as my leave would allow." Frowning, he shook his head. "It's still never enough, though."

"No, it's not," Kade agreed. A wry smile curved his lips as he told him, "I was in the military, but it was a good fifty years ago."

"Huh." Ronan hadn't thought Kade looked a day over thirty-five, but it seemed he'd forgotten to take into account that he was a shifter.

Kade returned his attention to the map on his tablet. "Let's try this route, then." He pointed to the right. "Take that side road. Then we'll need to find a discreet place to park. Once the sun starts to set, we'll be going for a short hike."

"Sounds good." Dixon took the turn indicated. A few

minutes later, he muttered, "Ah, here's a good spot." He turned the SUV into an area between a few trees, which quickly took them to the right and then to a dead end. "Bet it's a make-out spot."

"Well, that's not what we're using it for," Kade muttered, shaking his head. "I'd need Tom here for that."

Dixon snorted.

Ronan had heard that both wolf shifters were mated. Dixon's partner was a polar bear shifter named Helsinki, while Kade's lover was human. Both were waiting for them to return to Stone Ridge.

Turning in his seat, Kade tilted his tablet so everyone could see it. "We're here." He tapped the screen. Then he pointed elsewhere. "Your parents' home is here."

"There looks to be plenty of tree cover, plus it's cloudy to-night," Dixon pointed out. "We'll get there and back without too much difficulty."

Ronan sure as hell hoped so. He would hate to put any of his new friends in danger. To that end, he offered, "If it's a choice between me and saving yourselves, you should —"

"Don't finish that," Dixon growled just as a snarl erupted from Markus.

Kade sneered. "We don't leave our pack-mates behind."

Opening his mouth, Ronan intended to try again. He saw the hard looks on each of the men's faces. Meeting Markus's gaze, he noticed a good deal of frustration mixed in, too.

Cradling Markus's jaw, Ronan told him, "I don't want you getting hurt because of me."

"I wouldn't be getting hurt because of you, Ro," Markus insisted. "I'd be getting hurt because of some asshole follow-ing orders for another asshole."

Ronan nodded as he muttered softly, "This world is full of assholes."

Kade barked a laugh. "You got that right, man."

Ignoring the pair up front, Ronan dipped his head and pressed his lips to Markus's. He lapped at his lover's gently, in no hurry to deepen the kiss. Knowing they had an audience, he kept it light, all about reconnecting and reaffirming their bond.

After a few moments, Ronan lifted his head and smiled at Markus. "Thanks . . . for everything."

Markus shrugged. "I haven't done much."

Ronan shook his head, disagreeing. "You've given me hope for another way."

Not bothering to answer, Markus snuggled into his side. Ronan relaxed in the seat, holding his lover close. The others got comfortable, too, Dixon reading a book on his phone and Kade tapping away at his phone. The smile on his face when his phone vibrated ever-so-quietly told Ronan that it was probably a message from his partner.

Taking advantage of the quiet and putting his faith in the others, Ronan focused on relaxing.

To his surprise, he managed to slip into a light doze.

The tap against his calf brought Ronan to full wakefulness in an instant. He cracked an eyelid, surprised to see that the sun was nearly set. Long shadows dominated the area, attesting to the late hour.

"How long was I out?" Ronan asked.

"About an hour and a half," Dixon replied, confirming Ronan's suspicion. "You ready for a hike?"

Ronan nodded as Markus stretched beside him. "Let's get this done."

"Be careful and stay alert, everyone," Dixon ordered as they all slipped from the vehicle.

Unable to help himself, as Ronan started creeping through the forest after the pair, he grabbed onto Markus's hand. He squeezed lightly once, then released him. If anything happened to his lover, Ronan would never forgive himself—that included physical and mental health.

Gods, please let my family be accepting.

As Ronan watched Dixon flank left and Kade move to the right, he knew his job was to stay near the middle. He crept between trees, under brush, and over logs. Keeping an eye on his point-men, Ronan moved left and right as necessary, avoiding not only light from windows but keeping them downwind to neighborhood dogs.

He had to admit, having someone on the team with a super sniffer was damn convenient. He sort of understood why a scientist would try to give a soldier that ability. Still, while it could be useful in certain situations, there were plenty of others where it would be a detriment—like walking through a sewer or changing a diaper.

Talk about torture.

Ronan idly wondered how the shifters managed it.

They must just be used to it.

Spotting the windows of his family home through the trees to his left, Ronan refocused his attention. He peered at Dixon through the trees and noticed the man's signal for him to stay put. While Ronan couldn't crouch due to his brace and knee, he did slip behind a tree to wait.

The feel of Markus pressed against his side, his hand rubbing up and down his back soothingly, warmed him from the inside out.

Markus squeezed Ronan's upper arm, then pointed to the right. Following his lover's indication, he sought out Kade. He spotted the man tucked behind a tree.

As soon as Kade met Ronan's gaze, he gave him a thumbs up. Seeking out Dixon once more, Ronan saw the beta giving him a *go ahead* sign.

As swiftly as Ronan could, he jog-limped across the short expanse from the trees to his parents' back deck. Striding up the ten stairs, he grimaced at the pain shooting up his leg. Too much time in vehicles followed by running through the forest was not making his knee any happier.

I'll be able to rest it soon enough.

The lingering smell of cooked meat in the air told Ronan that his father had been grilling something.

"Mmm," Markus muttered softly. "Steaks. Strips, if I'm not mistaken."

Arching a brow, Ronan hissed, "You can figure out a cut by scent?"

Markus grinned and shrugged. "Unless they season it with something, yeah."

Ronan chuckled under his breath as he gripped the sliding glass door's handle. When he tugged, it opened. He rolled his eyes, wondering how many times he would need to tell his family to lock the sliding glass door.

"Trusting," Markus mumbled, shaking his head.

"Too trusting," Ronan countered as he eased inside. "Lock it."

Markus nodded before doing as he'd been told, sliding the latch down to lock it.

Turning, Ronan listened. He heard the TV on too loud in the downstairs family room, attesting to the fact that his father was starting to lose his hearing. Taking a deep, steadying breath, he prepared himself for what was to come.

Glancing around at the scuffed up dining room table and the faded wallpaper in the kitchen to the left, Ronan wondered if his parents would ever be able to return.

Assuming they leave with me.

Only one way to find out.

"Mom?" Ronan hesitated a second, then shouted, "Pops?"

For a second, nothing happened. Then the TV muted. "You call me, honey?" his father hollered.

Before Ronan could reply, the thud of footsteps on the

stairs cascaded through the house. His sister reached the bottom and used the railing to sling-shot around to face him. With a screech, she launched toward Ronan.

"Ronan!" Isabel cried. "You're here!"

Having every faith in him, Isabel jumped into his arms.

Refusing to disappoint her, Ronan caught his younger sister. When she wrapped her arms around his waist, giving him all her weight to support, his knee screamed. A second later, Ronan felt Markus grip the back of his belt loops, lending support and his strength.

"What on earth is going on up there?" his father called.

"Ronan's here!" Isabel yelled as she dropped back to her feet. She finally must have spotted Markus, for she froze, her hazel eyes going wide. "Oh, um. Hello."

Markus released Ronan's pants and stepped to his right. "Hi, I'm Markus. You must be Isabel." He held out his hand. "Ronan has told me so much about you."

"Hello," Isabel replied, taking his hand. As soon as they released, she tugged at the hem of her oversized sweater, revealing her discomfort. "Um." With blushing cheeks, she refocused on Ronan. "How long are you staying? Mom didn't say you were coming."

"Mom didn't know," Ronan told her, squeezing her shoulder. "Where is she?"

"In her sewing room," Isabel told him. "I'll go get her."

Then Isabel bounded away and headed back upstairs.

If Ronan had to guess, he would bet that his sister would also change into a nicer shirt, too. She only wore the oversized sweaters or sweatshirts when she thought there was only family around. While it had been about ten months, the last he'd talked to his mom, she'd confided that Isabel liked to wear stuff in front of others that showed off her developing breasts.

In truth, it had been more than Ronan had wanted to know

about his sister, but he'd tried to be supportive whenever his mother expressed concern about his siblings. Plus, he knew she expected him to have a talk to Isabel about staying away from boys. Ronan had never gotten the chance before he'd discovered where the military had transferred Bailey.

"Well, hot damn," a deep voice similar to his own sounded through the dining room. "Ronan!"

Limping forward, Ronan closed the distance to Greg Dyer. "Hi, Pops." He gave the slightly smaller man a bear hug. "It's damn good to see you."

"Well, let me look at you, son." His pops eased the hug and rested his hands on Ronan's shoulders. He looked him up and down, his attention snagging on his braced knee for a few seconds. When he met Ronan's gaze again, concern filled his brown eyes. Except, what he said was, "There were men here sayin' some troublin' things about ya, Ronan. Then we couldn't get in touch with ya. What's going on?"

Grimacing, Ronan nodded. "I can only guess at what they're claiming. That's why I've been away for so long. To keep you safe."

"Your ma and me figured as much," his pops told him. Tipping his chin at Ronan's leg, he stated, "Doesn't look like you're takin' care of yourself, boy. Irritate your war injury?"

"Afraid so," Ronan confirmed. With a shrug, he admitted, "Being on the run from the military isn't easy sometimes, but now I have help to sort out these lies."

"Bein' on the run?" his pops asked, his brows furrowing, betraying confusion Ronan didn't understand. Then his father noticed Markus behind him and asked, "Oh, is this a military friend?"

Markus stepped forward, his hand out. "No, not in the military." Then a small shadow fell over his face. "Well, not for a long time now, anyway."

Barely managing to school his features, Ronan knew he

and Markus needed to have a conversation. He hadn't known that at some point in his near one hundred and forty years, his lover had served in someone's military.

After the men exchanged greetings and names, his pops turned back to him. "Okay, son. What's goin' on?"

Knowing it was now or never — his father had always been a little mellower about his orientation — Ronan cleared his throat and stated, "Markus Reussmin is my partner, and he and our friends are helping me clear my name." Even as he saw his pops' brows shoot up his forehead, Ronan continued, "But what's going on with me is putting you in danger, too. I came because I'm worried about you." After a second, Ronan added, "And it involves Bailey."

The blood drained from his father's face, and his eyes widened. He shook his head. "You mean you haven't heard?" he asked in a rough whisper. "Ronan, Bailey passed away six months ago."

CHAPTER ELEVEN

Markus spotted the confusion on Ronan's face. Between one heartbeat and the next, he realized what was going on. His mate's parents had been lied to.

Grabbing Ronan's wrist, Markus drew his lover's attention. "Ronan, I think we need to have this conversation with both your parents." Upon seeing Ronan's nod, he refocused on Greg. "This is going to come as a shock. Perhaps we should all sit down?"

His confusion evident, Greg glanced between them. "What are you—"

"Oh, my goodness." A woman with short, curly gray hair stopped in the doorway. "Ronan, you're here!" Whatever shock the grandmotherly looking woman was experiencing, she must have gotten over it swiftly. With a soft cry of delight, she rushed to Ronan and threw her arms around him. "Oh, Ronan."

Ronan held her tightly, and Markus realized the lady had to be his mother. His mate confirmed that by bending his massive frame to hug the barely five-foot-five woman to him and saying, "Hi, Mom. It's so great to see you."

For several minutes, his mother trembled in Ronan's arms, and his mate whispered words of reassurance to her.

Gods, I hope learning that they'd been lied to doesn't make either of his parents' hearts go out.

When Markus thought of his own mother, who had died at three-hundred-eight-seven after their father had passed at five-hundred-twenty-two, she'd still been pretty damn spry.

If there hadn't been such an age gap, he bet she would have lived another one hundred years. Unfortunately, if a fated mate died, the other followed pretty swiftly.

The woman before him, however, seemed to be showing her age at a little over sixty. The last year had obviously been very difficult for her.

Feeling a hand on his arm, Markus focused on Greg.

"Let's give them a moment, hmm?" Greg murmured. "We'll start some tea." His eyes narrowed as he asked, "Or do we need to send Isabel back upstairs and pull out something stronger?"

Markus opened his mouth, then closed it again. He spotted Isabel standing nearby, appearing uncertain. She'd changed into a form-fitting, long-sleeved sweater and now had flats on her feet instead of slippers.

Huh.

"Gods, sir," Markus muttered. "I wish I knew."

"A fair answer," Greg stated, pointing toward the kitchen. "We'll start with tea. Shall we? I know Victoria would appreciate that."

Markus nodded and followed Greg's lead. Obeying the man's instructions, he helped him put a kettle on for tea. Then they found tea bags. Markus chose a bag for himself. Then, recalling Ronan's fondness for mint, he picked an herbal mint tea for his lover.

To Markus's pleasure, he noted the impressed look on Greg's face, so he must have chosen well.

The whistling of the teapot seemed to help Victoria pull herself together. She stepped away from Ronan, patting his arm. Then she bustled into the kitchen, wiping her eyes on her sleeve before turning to the sink.

"I'm so sorry you had to see that," Victoria claimed as she washed her hands. "It's just, it's been such a tough year. I—" As she dried her hands, her eyebrows furrowed. "I'm sorry, dear. Who are you?"

Ronan was there in an instant, reaching for his hand. "Mother, this is Markus Reussmin. He and his friends are helping me clear my name." After a second of hesitation, Ronan added, "He's my partner."

"P-Partner?" Victoria stuttered. She glanced from Ronan to her husband and back again. After blinking a few times, she murmured, "I see." Drying her hands, Victoria added, "I suppose we never really did talk about your . . . well, *that* much, did we?" Sighing, she added, "I had just hoped you'd, well, grown out of the phase."

"Mom, being gay isn't a phase," Isabel stated, cocking her head and sounding confused. "You know that."

"But for him to spring *this* on us *now?*" Victoria countered, shaking her head as she moved to Greg's side. "Don't you think we've had enough to deal with this year?"

"Ronan's introducing us to someone important in his life, Victoria," Greg stated, wrapping his arm around his wife's waist. "And he didn't know about Bailey, dear. You know he's been in holding by the military police. They wouldn't even let us see him."

The lies just keep getting better and better.

Blowing out a deep breath, Ronan shook his head. "I think we all need to sit down."

"Good idea," his father confirmed. Turning, he grabbed the teapot, then began pouring water into each mug. "I chose a decaf English breakfast for you, Isabel. I hope you don't mind. We didn't have any more spiced chai."

"That's fine," Isabel said softly, taking the mug. "Thanks, Pops."

"Here, dear." Greg handed Victoria a mug containing some kind of fruity tea bag. "Let's go down and get comfortable in the family room."

Victoria glanced between Ronan and Markus before nodding.

As they left the room, Markus handed Ronan the mint tea

and picked up the orange flavored one he'd chosen.

"Sorry about that," Ronan whispered.

"No need to apologize," Markus murmured back. "Like she said, they've had a rough year, and from the sounds of it, they've been lied to about a few things."

"Now I don't know if I want to tell them," Ronan admitted, grimacing. "They've already grieved."

"And if Bailey wakes up and wants to see them?" Markus countered. "What are you going to tell him?"

Ronan groaned, tipping his head back. "Damn, I know you're right."

"Did I just hear you say something about Bailey waking up?"

Markus spotted Isabel loitering in the doorway. She nibbled her lower lip as her gaze darted between them.

Well, fuck.

"Whoever came and talked to you lied about a few things," Ronan stated softly as he crossed to Isabel. He wrapped his arm around her shoulders as he guided her downstairs after their parents. "I'll explain as best I can."

Then Ronan peered over his shoulder at Markus, and he hurried after his mate.

Ronan guided Isabel to a long sofa, settling in the middle. When he beckoned to Markus, he strode to him and sat beside him. Markus noticed his mate's parents were on a small sofa to their right, and the TV had been turned off.

"So, you believe that Bailey passed away, and that I was in a military cell somewhere," Ronan began slowly. He kept his arm around Isabel's shoulders even though he pressed his other shoulder into Markus, all the while balancing his tea on his thigh. "Neither of those things are true."

Evidently, Ronan was going with the *rip off the band-aid* approach.

Both his parents leaped to their feet, although it was apparent that Victoria was yelling at Ronan while Greg was trying to calm her down. His sister just whispered, "Really?" But the question was damn near drowned out by their parents. Only Markus's shifter hearing allowed him to catch it.

Reaching behind Ronan, Markus touched her shoulder, catching her attention. He nodded, offering her a small smile. Her big hazel eyes widened even further, welling up with tears that she did her best to blink away.

Markus took the next few seconds to type a quick message into his phone to Lark.

"Victoria, please," Greg pleaded, taking her tea from her hands and placing it on an end table beside his own. Then he gripped both her hands between his. "Just let him explain. You know our son would never purposefully be cruel. There must be a reason he claims such things."

Finally, Victoria sucked in a deep breath before letting it out between pursed lips. She nodded once, then allowed Greg to help her settle back on the love seat.

"I'm sorry, Mom," Ronan began. "I should have broached that better." He shook his head. "It was thoughtless of me." Glancing between his parents, Ronan claimed, "But I'm telling the truth. I found Bailey in a hidden base being experimented on by someone. I don't know how he ended up there or why the military is complicit in hiding him." Growling under his breath, Ronan grumbled, "It's like there's no honor in any group anymore. Corruption at all levels."

Rubbing Ronan's back, Markus whispered, "Focus, Ro. We'll ferret out these a—uh, jerks." Hearing Isabel snicker, he figured she'd heard his amendment.

Oh well. At least I brought her a little levity in this moment.

Ronan turned toward him and rested his forehead on Markus's shoulder. "Thanks," he muttered.

"Anytime," Markus replied just as softly. "Always and forever."

Lifting his head, Ronan smiled faintly at him. Then he

shocked the shit out of Markus by leaning forward and pecking a kiss to his lips. Still, when he did it a second time, Markus would never deny him, and he gently kissed him back.

A loud, obnoxious, "Uh-hum!" filled the room.

Ronan eased back, a pleading expression in his dark eyes.

Markus smiled faintly, hoping his look conveyed his understanding.

Returning his focus to his parents, Ronan told them, "I snuck Bailey out of that facility over nine months ago, but he was in a coma. Since I knew the military was in on it, I hid Bailey with Corporal Haas. He's been taking care of him." Then Ronan glanced Markus's way before explaining, "Until yesterday, when Markus's people took him to one of their homes hidden in the mountains. Brian is there, too, but Markus's friends have had experience with whatever the hell was done to Bailey." His deep voice croaking, Ronan stated, "I finally have hope that he might make it."

Finally running out of steam, Ronan took a swig of his mint tea.

"A-Are you saying that B-Bailey is alive, but you're not sure he's going to live?" Victoria squeaked.

When Ronan didn't get a sound out, Markus took over. Softly, he confirmed, "That's exactly what he's saying. He didn't know you already thought he was dead. He didn't know you weren't aware that Ronan was running for his life these last nine months." Scoffing softly, Markus shook his head. "He would have been so tempted to allow you to believe those lies, since you seemed to be moving on from this trauma, but what happens when Bailey wakes up and you're not there for him as he recovers?"

Gods, what will happen if – when – Bailey wakes up and he does start to recover . . . as a shifter?

What a mess!

Markus watched as Victoria and Greg exchanged a look.

Ronan's mother had tears running down her cheeks, while his father's bushy gray brows were furrowed in concern. His mate just continued to drink his tea, obviously at a loss for words.

Markus's phone chimed. He looked down to see a return message from Lark. Opening it, he saw what he wanted—a picture of Bailey asleep in one of the medical rooms Lark had created on the second floor of the alpha and alpha-mate's home.

After showing it to Ronan, who nodded, Markus tilted the phone and showed it to Isabel. She gasped and grabbed it. With a hand over her mouth, she asked thickly, "When?"

"Just now," Markus answered quietly. "Doctor Lark Trystan just sent that to me. I trust him with my life."

Her hand still over her mouth, her focus completely on Markus's phone, Isabel rose to her feet. She slowly made her way across the room. Somehow, she managed to wedge between her parents on the small sofa, sitting between them.

"Bailey's alive," Isabel whispered. "Look!"

Both parents stared at the phone for several long minutes.

While they did that, Markus rubbed Ronan's back. He smiled reassuringly when his lover turned to look at him once more. He smiled back at him, warming Markus from the inside out.

"S-So what's wrong with B-Bailey?" Greg asked huskily, obviously fighting emotion.

"That's a bit of a loaded question," Markus answered honestly. "If you want to know the truth, there are conditions."

"What sort of conditions," Victoria demanded. "This is my son. I deserve to know!"

Ronan turned his attention back to his parents with a weary sigh. "I've been running from the people who did that to Bailey for nine months, Mom. As long as you knew nothing, they had no reason to hurt you to get information." Once again, he went with the blunt approach. "These are people willing to hold others against their will. They'd experiment on them." He glanced between the three of them as he murmured, "If you want to know, you can't stay here. You have to come with us. You have to go into protection so you'll be kept safe."

"I—You—We—" Victoria broke off trying to convey her thoughts. Her pale blue eyes were wide behind her glasses, and she looked beyond shell-shocked.

"I'll go." Isabel jumped to her feet and hurried back to Ronan's side. "Anything for Bailey."

Greg patted Victoria's hand as he smiled tightly at Ronan and Markus. "We will, too. It's the right thing to do. We'll never abandon our children." He returned his attention to Victoria, whispering, "No matter what."

Victoria took in a tremulous breath, then a second one, before a soft smile curved her lips. "No matter what."

"Good!" The deep voice boomed through the room as a man in military fatigues stalked into view. He carried a handgun in his right hand and a walkie-talkie in his other as he surveyed the group with a cold-eyed gaze. "Now you can take all of us to Bailey."

Two more men in camo pants and black long-sleeved shirts and carrying guns followed the first, fanning out and training their weapons on them.

Victoria gasped, while Greg stiffened. Ronan leaned forward, pushing Isabel behind him. He tried to do the same to Markus, but Markus wouldn't let him.

Lifting the walkie-talkie to his mouth, the lead stranger stated, "We've found Ronan, Professor. We'll have the location of his brother soon."

"Good," a voice crackled through the line. "I want experiment ZX-thirty-two back as soon as possible. By my calculations, he should be entering the final stages."

Well, shit.

CHAPTER TWELVE

Two against three. Those were going to be some tough odds.

Still, Ronan had to try. From the way Markus had refused to be pushed behind him with Isabel, his lover planned to make a move, too. Of course, that would have been a little awkward on the sofa anyway. He just wished his parents weren't so damn far away.

"Markus, what do you think?" Ronan began softly. "Guess he's the asshole we need to take in for questioning, huh?"

"Yup," Markus replied softly. "He's the guy." Cocking his head, he asked the man with the walkie-talkie, "Sooo, who's the professor you're talking to? What final stages are you talking about?"

Ronan sure as hell hoped the final stage wasn't death. If he'd offered his parents and sister hope for no reason, he would end up going on a killing spree. He vowed to hunt down every last one of these bastards and splatter their brains all over whatever wall was closest.

Not surprisingly, the man didn't reply to Markus's queries. "Tell me where you're hiding your brother," the man demanded instead.

"Why do you want to know?" Ronan asked with a growl.

As if I don't already know.

Narrowing his eyes, the man swung his gun to the left until he pointed the weapon at Ronan's parents. "Try again."

"Wait." Markus slowly rose to his feet, his hands lifted in placation. "There's no need to threaten the old couple. They don't know where he is."

"But Ronan does," the man countered. "So do you." A cruel smirk curved his lips. "Here's what's going to happen. I'm going to count backward from five. If neither of you tell me where you've stashed the professor's experiment, I'm going to kill the old man." He grinned evilly. "Five seconds after that. Pow."

The guy fake-shot Victoria, causing Ronan's mother to whimper and cringe harder against Greg.

A low growl rumbled from Markus, just low enough for Ronan to hear. He glanced at his lover, surprise filling him when he saw the feral snarl curving his lips. His hands were clenched, and he gritted his teeth.

The asshole wasn't done.

"After that, I'll just pop you both and take that sweet young thing back to the professor. He'll be pissed to start over, but whatever." After a negligent shrug, he added with a leer, "That'll be after we have a bit of fun with her first, though."

Just as Ronan heard Isabel whimper, two other things happened at once. The lead gunman called out, "Five," starting his countdown, just as something crashed through both of the room's windows.

"What the fuck!" one of the other armed men screamed.

In the next instant, Markus was gone from Ronan's side. The sound of snarls filled the room. There was cracking and popping and screams, yells, and roars.

Ronan jumped to his feet as best he could and lunged at the speaker. As he grabbed the man's hand, he spotted the blurs of blond and black fur as wolves streaked past him. The blast of a gunshot reverberated through the room, and his ears rang.

Slamming his full weight into the slimmer man, Ronan drove him backward. The man's calves hit the stairs, and he tumbled, Ronan landing on top of him.

When Ronan's knee hit the stair, he roared as pain surged

through his leg. He channeled the agony into adrenaline. Using every ounce of strength he had in his bicep, he slammed the gunman's wrist into the step.

The man grunted, but he didn't drop the weapon, so Ronan did it again . . . and again . . .

Just as the guy's fingers loosened and he lost his grip, Ronan spotted him bringing up his other arm, which held a knife. He arched his back, narrowly missing his swipe. Crunching his abdominals, Ronan came back twice as fast and with a fist.

Ronan slammed his left hand into the gunman's face as hard as he could. He heard the crunch of bone. Pain flared through his fingers. Blood sprayed from the man's nose, splashing across the wall and all over his hand.

Drawing his arm back, Ronan prepared to hit him again, but someone caught his arm. He twisted sideways, ready for the next fight. Except . . . the blond standing over him was naked. He also had his hands up in a placating move.

"Relax, Ronan," the man ordered. "He's unconscious. He's not going anywhere."

"Dixon?" Ronan whispered, trying to gather his senses.

"I was the blond wolf," Dixon rumbled softly. He slowly lowered his left hand and pointed at the black wolf sitting near the two downed men. "That's Kade. He'll guard all the fallen. You need to go calm your family now." After a second of hesitation, Dixon added, "And Markus needs you."

"Markus?" Ronan whispered, trying to sort his thoughts. He suddenly recalled that his lover had lunged toward his parents. "What happened?"

Even before Dixon could answer, Ronan spotted what he meant. A strawberry blond wolf lay sprawled on the family room floor before the sofa his parents had been seated on. His parents were behind the piece of furniture and had their arms around Isabel, physically restraining her as she tried to get to the animal.

"He saved us," Isabel cried, struggling against them. "We have to help him."

"He attacked us," Victoria countered, holding onto her daughter's arm. "It was a coincidence." Then she glared at Dixon as she even tried to cover Isabel's eyes.

Ronan shoved to his feet, but his knee gave out. Even the brace didn't save him. Fortunately, Dixon caught him, keeping him from going down.

"Get your balance on that chair," Dixon ordered. "I gotta release you so I can grab the throw blanket." With a soft snort, he added, "I think I'm traumatizing your mother."

"At least my sister isn't paying you any mind," Ronan muttered through gritted teeth as he did as Dixon ordered.

Dixon snorted, then released him and snagged the throw off the back of the sofa so he could wrap it around himself toga-style.

Resting his right hand on the back of the chair, Ronan began half-hopping, half-limping around it so he could reach the wolf he knew was Markus. He eased down beside his lover in wolf form, reaching out to him. The animal whined and flopped its tail once. It stared up at him with pain-filled hazel eyes.

That was when Ronan spotted the blood oozing from its torso.

"Oh, babe," Ronan murmured. "What were you thinking?"

"He threw himself between Mom and Pops and that guy with the gun," Isabel told him over Victoria's protests. "He saved them."

Ronan gently laid his hand on Markus's neck, stroking softly. "Relax, babe," he urged, smiling at the beast. "You'll be fine. I'll get ya help." Then Ronan turned his attention to his mother. "You can let Isabel go, Mom. None of these shifters will hurt you."

Victoria clutched Isabel tighter, her eyes full of accusation. "You brought these monsters into our house. Why would you do that if you knew those violent men were after them?" Her voice tightened as she added, "You should have left us out of it. You should have come to us alone instead of bringing trouble."

"Bailey wouldn't have a snowball's chance in hell of surviving without these monsters," Ronan roared, interrupting his mother. "They saved me, and now they're trying to save Bailey!"

Hearing Markus whimper, Ronan turned his attention to his lover. He stroked his fur around his ears, doing his best to soothe him. Turning, he glanced around just as Dixon dropped to his knees beside him.

"How is he?" Dixon asked.

"Hell if I know," Ronan replied with a grimace. "I don't know shit about the health of you all."

Dixon chuckled as he nodded. "Okay. Fair enough." He scratched Markus's honey-blond haunch as he stated, "You stay with us, Markus. I'm not going to answer to your brother if anything happens to you. Got it?"

Markus whimpered and thumped his tail again.

"Let's see here." Dixon began carefully separating the fur around the oozing wound, checking placement. After a few seconds, he claimed, "If we can get that bullet out of him, he'll heal up just fine."

"I'm in a preliminary veterinary course," Isabel called. "I started this past year. I can help."

"You are certainly not helping that animal," Victoria countered, still holding her in a tight grip. "Didn't you see what happened? Ronan's boyfriend turned into that *thing*. It's an abom—"

"Enough!" Ronan roared. "Don't even think about finishing that sentence, Mom." He pointed at his mother. "You're not happy about me being gay, fine, but you better get it through your head right now." Ronan pointed at his lover. "If Bailey pulls through, he could turn out to be just like one of these shifters. And these guys weren't after any of these men. They were after *me*, and they were after *Bailey*."

Victoria's eyes widened. Her hands flew to her mouth.

Isabel took advantage and sprinted around the sofa. Dropping to her knees, she took a quick look before saying, "We won't be able to see anything with all this hair in the way." In the next second, she was back on her feet. "I'll get Dad's shaver."

Markus whined with annoyance, sounding completely put out.

Chuckling, Dixon shook his head. "It's not the worst thing that could happen to you." Then he patted Ronan. "Trust me. Once the bullet is out, Markus will heal swiftly enough."

Ronan nodded, taking Dixon's word for it. Lifting his focus to his parents, he saw the way his dad held his mother close. Except, when their gazes met, his pops smiled a little, pride filling his eyes.

His pops nodded once, then turned a fond gaze on the wolf sprawled on the floor.

Relief flooded Ronan. He knew with his father's backing, his mom would come around. That was how it had always been. His father was the calm, steady waters while his mother had been the reactive firecracker. He put out her flames, and she kept a little spice in his life.

Perfect together, just like Markus and me.

Then Isabel dropped beside him, a razor in her hands, and Ronan focused on helping his lover.

Once they'd removed the bullet and bandaged the wound, Ronan eased Markus's head onto his lap. He gently teased his fingers through his fur as he watched his lover change from beast to man. Dixon was immediately there with another blanket, covering his nudity.

With a soft groan, Markus muttered, "Ow."

Ronan snorted. "Really? That's all you have to say?"

Markus peered up at him and arched one brow. "You're welcome?"

Tipping his head back, Ronan laughed for a moment. When he refocused on his lover, he dipped his head and gave him an awkward kiss.

"Damn, babe. You're going to keep me on my toes, aren't you?"

Markus grinned up at him, although his appeared a little pained. "I'll always try."

"I look forward to it."

"Time to load everything into the SUV," Dixon stated from where he stood nearby. "Kade took off and snagged it while you finished up with Markus. Your parents are packing." With a wink, he added, "Don't worry. Your father is supervising. They'll be following us in their own *Suburban*. Your sister and father will have plenty of time to get your mom to come around."

Ronan nodded. "I know she will." He met Markus's gaze and held it. "Like they said before. They'll never abandon their children."

"What about you, Ro?" Markus asked softly. "Want children?"

Rolling his eyes, Ronan shook his head. "How about we discuss that when we're both back on our feet?"

Markus reached up and cupped the back of his neck. "It's a deal."

Then Markus drew Ronan down, and he was happy to seal that vow with a kiss.

You may also enjoy the following from eXtasy Books Inc:

A Wolf in Hiding
Charlie Richards

Excerpt

As Elroy drove, he shot off a text to Bart.

I'm headed out. What's your ETA?

Since Bart lived closer to the trailhead than Elroy did and they'd already planned to be there in the neighborhood of two PM, he figured his buddy would be waiting—probably with questions about his lunch with Camilla.

When Elroy didn't get a response right away, he placed his phone in the cup holder. He enjoyed the scenic drive along the winding roads, through the small town of Stone Ridge, and finally into the forested mountains. If his job hadn't been in the heart of Colin City, he would have bought a place closer to nature.

Elroy arrived at the trailhead and parked his car. To his surprise, he still hadn't heard from Bart. He picked up his phone, pleased to discover he still had a signal.

Dialing his friend's number, Elroy brought the phone to his ear.

"Hello?" Bart sounded distracted.

"Hey, Bart," Elroy greeted. "I'm at the trailhead, ready and waiting. When—"

Bart's cussing interrupted Elroy. "Ah, damn, man. I am so sorry." His tone held a wealth of regret and frustration. "Laura called in a panic because Nate crashed his bike and hurt himself, and Mark has the car for work. She needed a ride to take Nate to the hospital, and I . . . I shoulda called, but—" Groaning under his breath, Bart ran out of steam.

Even as disappointment flooded him, Elroy nodded in understanding. "It's okay, Bart. Really," he assured his friend. "Family comes first."

Elroy had met Bart's sister, Laura, on many occasions, and she was warm and accepting, not batting an eyelash when she discovered he was gay. Their ten-year-old son, Nate, was a great kid, if a little hyper at times. Mark worked hard as an electrician, owning his own company, so it wasn't a surprise that he would work the occasional Saturday.

After another deep sigh, Bart murmured, "I'm sorry I forgot to call you."

Leaning his head back against the headrest, Elroy closed his eyes. "Stop apologizing, Bart," he ordered, keeping his tone soothing. "Is Nate okay?"

"He will be. Sprained his right wrist."

"That won't slow him down for long." Elroy felt confident of that.

Bart chuckled softly. "You know it." After a couple of heartbeats of silence, he told him, "I'm still at the hospital. They should be discharged soon, but—"

"Hey. Relax, man." Elroy didn't care for the self-flagellation in Bart's tone. His buddy was too upbeat to sound so defeated. "We'll catch this trail another time."

"You're not goin' then?" Bart didn't let Elroy answer before adding, "Aren't you already there?"

"Yeah, but I've never hiked this trail before, and it's a strenuous one." Elroy didn't want to admit to being worried about hiking alone. "I think I'll head to Condor's Point trailhead and enjoy something a little more leisurely that I've done before."

"All right. Probably a good idea," Bart conceded. "We'll try for next weekend." He cleared his throat before saying, "Let me know how I can make it up to ya."

Elroy's first inclination was to reply, "Don't worry about it." Instead, he smiled. "You have plans for tomorrow afternoon?"

"Not currently."

An idea formed, and he grinned.

"You can come over and help me clean out my car." Elroy conveniently left out the part where Camilla would be there, too.

And I won't tell her, either.

If Elroy could get the pair working together for any length of time, he just knew they'd get over their shyness and actually have a conversation which could lead to a date.

"Sure, man," Bart replied. "You got it."

"Okay. I'll text you a time later," Elroy told him. "Go be with your family."

"Have a safe hike," Bart replied. "Bye."

"Later."

Elroy hung up, placed his phone in the cup holder, and restarted his engine. Then he headed toward the other trailhead.

Three hours later, Elroy decided Bart's order about having a safe hike had jinxed him. Pain radiated through his left leg, and his head throbbed. He barely felt the shivers from the flash thunderstorm that had drenched him.

That's not good.

With his arms wrapped around his torso, Elroy sat on the wet ground and forced his eyelids open. He slowly panned his gaze over the forest around him. Then he peered up and behind him.

Breathing deeply, Elroy barely kept the spots dancing across his vision at bay.

Elroy had no idea where he was.

After getting turned around by the heavy rainstorm, making visibility next to nil, Elroy had figured hunkering down was his best option. He'd tried to search for a thicket or thick stand of trees to hide in. Instead, the undergrowth he'd chosen had hidden a cliff.

Between one step and the next, Elroy had fallen right over it.

When Elroy had landed, he'd screamed as his left leg snapped under him. He'd buckled, his right arm catching some of his weight and scraping over rocks. That pain caused him to twist, and he'd slammed his head against the cliff.

Elroy didn't know how he'd managed to stay conscious, but he'd done it. He slowly, carefully, eased to a sitting position, fighting the waves of nausea caused by the agony shooting through his leg. Having broken his arm once in the past, he recognized that kind of pain.

Leaning against the cliff face, Elroy panted softly. The spots increased even as the rain slacked off and stopped. Every shudder of his body brought fresh waves of debilitating throbs.

Elroy whimpered upon seeing the blood seeping through the left leg of his jeans. With a shaky left hand, he pulled his cell phone from his jacket pocket.

The cracked screen told him all he needed to know, but he tried waking it anyway.

Broken.

Taking a deep breath, Elroy used all his strength to bellow, "Hello?"

No answer.

Elroy gritted his teeth for several moments, then tried again.

Still nothing.

Unable to help himself, Elroy felt his eyes water as fear slithered through his veins.

"I'm gonna die out here," Elroy whispered, his heart clenching in his chest. The spots across his vision intensified as a wave of dizziness swept over him, caused by either blood loss or fear. He wasn't certain which.

Movement to his right caught his attention, and he blinked, barely able to focus on it.

"No way," Elroy mumbled as his heart rate spiked for a new reason.

A medium brown wolf padded toward him.

At least I won't die of exposure.

That was Elroy's last thought as he gave in to the pain, and his eyes rolled to the back of his head as he passed out.

About the Author

Charlie started writing fantasy when she was eight, and after stumbling onto her first erotic romance at age nineteen, she realized her true calling. She now focuses on writing gay erotic romance, normally of the paranormal variety, with heroes of all kinds. With the help and support of her husband, Charlie finally fulfilled one of her life-long goals . . . move to acreage with her horses. You can often find her curled up with her laptop and a cup of tea or glass of wine, creating her next adventure. Charlie enjoys exploring the mountains of her new Oregon home on horseback, 4-wheeler, or motorcycle.

She can be reached at ch.richards2010@yahoo.com
Or visit her at www.charlie-richards.com

www.ingramcontent.com/pod-product-compliance
Lightning Source LLC
Chambersburg PA
CBHW070455130626
46555CB00003B/1015